A Saunter With Death

Book 1: Kmoneiethe's Saga

Z. Halferty

To the one that flips me off on a daily basis.

Zombie '14

24 of 24

ISBN-10: 1497500222

ISBN-13: 978-1497500228

I dedicate this book to my beautiful daughter, loving wife, and all those that pushed me to finish my work and those that have made a difference in my life. Thank you all.

Fuck you guys!

Log Entry 1

It has been three days since the news broke. I did not hesitate as I grabbed my equipment and barricaded the door with the couch. Using a hammer, nails, and several pieces of wood, I boarded the windows, doors, and any other orifice I could find. Once every opening in the house was secured, I retreated to the second floor. I removed several of the steps on my way up, tearing them from their foundations as I went. I had ensured that I had enough equipment with me.

In my supplies I had plenty of food and water to last months. I also had several weapons; among these was a .22 rifle with thousands of rounds. I examined everything as though there was an intruder behind every structure. Tediously, I searched every aperture and every crevice possible. After all was cleared, I began to relax some. I had a large survival knife strapped to my right leg, several throwing knives wrapped around my left, and two heavy machetes, hanging from my belt, in the rear as though they were the tails of a penguin suit.

I found this notebook in one of the closets up here. I thought it would help me keep sane if I wrote everything at the end of each day. I will keep a log as consistently as possible as I attempt to record my struggle. Unfortunately, I do not know what day it is nor do I have any sense of time as the sun does not shine through the barricades. I will not try to estimate, for it would be of no use. I instead will attempt to recount, in immense detail, the events of each day.

Three days ago, the news broke of an attack, like no other anyone has ever witnessed. A man had ripped the jugular vein of a woman from her neck using only his teeth. He then, commenced to eating the flesh of the woman. Police arrived as the woman began to convulse, spitting blood all over them. They fired at the man several times, hitting him in vital areas, none of which seemed to do any harm. Only when an officer fired a shotgun round into the man's chest did he react. After four more shots, three of them to the heart, the man stopped and simply fell to the ground. The woman was rushed to the hospital, where she later died.

The police officers went to the hospital for tests to be run, to ensure they did not contract a disease. After blood was drawn, they all returned home. The medical staff had attempted to test the blood several times, only to find the system kept replying with error messages. The officers were seen the next morning, running down the streets, chasing different people in whichever neighborhood they had stayed the night. Many of them were covered in, what witnesses say, blood. None of them seemed to respond when spoken to. Instead they acted as though they were rabid animals.

A large police task force was called in to contain the situation. They were followed by the Center for Disease Control and Prevention (CDC). All seemed well as the victims and the officers were transported to the hospital. The victims were taken to critical care, while the officers were restrained. The medical staff attempted several times to treat them, many of which were bitten or assaulted with a spray of blood from the men's mouths. Due to the situation, the men were left to calm down, in hope that the fits of rage would pass.

They were ignorant. They did not know what they were dealing with. I did. I knew and I was prepared. They only saw what was happening locally. If they had paid attention, they may have caught on. This is a world-wide epidemic; we are the third country to experience the effects of this disease. They did not care; they did not want to believe that our government would not have control of such a situation.

It only took two days for the epidemic to spread through the major cities. People began to riot as absolute chaos broke out. Pure Anarchy swept across the nation as people fought to survive. Many died, not from the disease or the infected, but from the people that would do anything to survive even if only for a few minutes. Mothers left their children to die. Men fought over the simplest of things, whether it was a television or a beer. Gunshots rang out through the streets in every direction as people began to shoot one another, the police and military tried to get control of the population, and people committed suicide.

It was only two days before the military was overwhelmed. Everyone retreated, attempting to get to a safe location. Some hid in bunkers, others in stores, while others took to the sewers. The news had continued to broadcast through the entire event. People were dying at an extravagant rate, the infection was spreading like wildfire, and the infected were becoming too many in number to control.

All hope for humanity was lost. Those who did get away will not survive for long. And the few that do manage to survive are not going to be easy to find. To make things more difficult, on the second day, the power went out. I built a small fire; using a water pipe I ripped from the wall to funnel the smoke. I will just wait here until the pandemonium has deescalated, then I will move on.

Log Entry 2

The 'creatures' outside have been making a lot of noise. I do not know what is happening outside of these walls. I thought I heard a small child screaming earlier, but I could do nothing to aid them. After hearing the screams, I felt helpless, sick even. I knew there was nothing I could do but I did not even try to see what had happened. I know that there is nothing I can do now, but I may have been able to at least help the child get away, even if it would have been in vain.

After the screaming-child incident, I removed a portion of the barricade that covered an upper floor window. I peered out through the small opening, I would guess it to be nearly ten centimeters tall and maybe eight wide. Through it, I am able to extend my rifle and still focus through the scope. I have yet to examine the range that lies beyond the wall, but it is on the southeast side of the house. If my memory serves correct, this should allow me to see down the street toward town square. I feel no need to list the names of streets or towns for they will be of no use.

Once I had established a post near the opening, I covered it with a large sheet of linoleum I had removed from the bathroom floor; I feel this will allow me to open or close it as I choose, giving me a small window from which I can view the outside world; which will also allow for me to have some sense of days passing, and providing me with a 'sniper's nest.' The entire area around the opening is fortified with dense materials I had found strewn throughout this upper level and the attic. I feel this will help protect me if anyone attempted to return fire, which may be unlikely, but I am not taking a chance.

I have removed the bathtub; moving it into the room with the opening. I believe this will become my 'bunker' of sorts. I have set the tub against the wall just under the opening, thus, providing more protection from incoming fire, a place to sleep, and something similar to a fox hole in case something managed to get into the house. I also added several trip-lines across the top of the stairs, the doorways, and the corridors. I am trying to build a small wall in the center of the main corridor that leads to the different rooms, but have been unsuccessful in my search for durable materials. I did, however, find a large collection of storage trunks in the attic, they may make for a decent barricade; I believe there are eight or nine altogether.

Earlier today, there was a large crash outside as though someone had driven a vehicle into a wall or something. I cannot tell exactly where the sound came from but I do know it was close. Once it gets light out, I will attempt to see what the source was through the opening. I will also attempt to determine an escape route, for when it comes time to leave I want to know what my options are. I will also need to make a few more openings, just in case I may need to alter my plans. For now, I will try to get some sleep.

Log Entry 3

Last night was a sleepless one. The creatures outside made so much noise eating something, it kept me awake. The sound of bones breaking and flesh ripping would not leave my mind as I lay awake wondering what will be my fate. Once the creatures finished eating, they began to make noise similar to growls mixed with a horrid coughing noise. I could not see what they were doing but, from the sounds they were making, it seemed as though they were fighting.

Later in the night, something had been thrown at the opening. When I investigated, I found a partially eaten arm hanging just outside the window. It was dangling from an electrical line that connected to the house. I turned away, hiding, hoping they did not see me. After that incident, I wandered around the upper floor, wondering if there was a way I could get to the lower floor. I examined every centimeter of the remaining stairs, their railing, and the railing across the upper corridor. I decided that if I was careful, I should be able to but I first need to find something to help me get down and back up.

I removed portions of some of the barricades covering the windows. I searched everything, taking consideration of every possible escape route. I have not made a decision, yet, but I feel that my best option may be the southern-most window. I believe through it, I should be able to get to the roof, move from the roof to the fence connecting the house to the shed, and then go from there to the neighboring house, and so on. I cannot be sure until I explore some more. I also removed some of the paneling from one end of the attic; this made for a great 'sniper's nest,' allowing me to see the area in front of the house. According to my compass, it faces northwest. From there I can see the city, the massive buildings which line the streets there, and a portion of the interstate.

I have a clear view, through my scope, of the park from the new opening in the attic. There are several of those creatures walking around, slowly at first, until they see something to eat, then they are fast, really fast. I will have to take extra precautions if I want to make it out of this alive. There is no way I will be able to out run one, let alone a group of them, if I have even half of my equipment with me. I will have to leave most of my equipment behind; only taking what I absolutely need. This will make things a lot harder but I think I can make it through.

I found a piece of piping, last night, in the ceiling of the bathroom. It seems to be about fifteen meters long and stretches across most of the house's upper level. I hope that I can find a way to remove it without bending or damaging it. I believe if I manage to do so, I may be able to use it for several things; including balancing myself while walking across the fence. The pipe seems to be plenty long enough to reach the ground from the fence and I will be able to use it to lean against as I walk. I may also be able to fashion a hook onto the end of it, allowing me to reach things in the lower level and on the ground outside. I found a few items and a bag outside the southern-most opening. If I can reach them, they may be helpful. I will attempt to retrieve them tomorrow.

I also took an inventory, earlier. I am estimating that I have about two week's supply of food and two and a half week's supply of water. If I cannot find a new source of food and water soon, I will have to leave before my supply diminishes to nothing. Once I leave, I may not be able to return. Those creatures may follow me, thus I will not be able to stay here without them attempting to get in. From the sounds they have been making, they may already be trying to get in. I will attempt to examine the barricades, with a mirror fashioned to something, first thing tomorrow. For now, I cannot take any chances so I will be sleeping with my rifle across my chest.

Log Entry 4

Another sleepless night. The creatures outside made so much noise, it seemed as though they were tearing down the neighboring house. There were several screams. This time, I investigated, however, could not see who or what it was. I tried every opening trying to get a view of the source of the screams, but no luck. I continued to watch through the opening, altering every few moments, in hopes of catching a glimpse of someone running. I did not see anything living, other than those creatures.

I found a towel rack. It took a while before I managed to bend it; it is amazing, the effects of sleep deprivation. After I bent it into a U-shape, I tied some of the rope I had in my supplies to it. Using it, I attempted, and failed, several times to collect the bag and other items on the ground outside. I gave up after what seemed like hours and returned to the long pipe in the bathroom ceiling. It took until after nightfall to finally free the pipe without bending it too bad. Once I got it free, I held the 'hook' to the end, wrapped the rope around it several times and tied it off. After testing the hook's strength several times, I moved my new tool into the room from which I could see the bag and other items. I was too tired to try obtaining the bag again and instead left it there. I will try again as soon as I have the strength.

I accidentally spilled a few liters of water, cutting my supply down to two weeks. I will need to find a water source soon. I have placed all of my water supply in the bathtub and plugged the drain, hoping this will help prevent any more loss of water. I only have two week's supply of food left; if I ration it. I am very hungry and often wish to eat more but I know that is a major mistake. I will just have to suffer through this. At least until I can find more food but even then I know I will need to ration anything I find. I know that I may not be able to find more food so I must take caution when dealing with my food supply.

My leg is sore. I almost fell from the upper floor, when leaning over the railing, while trying to reach a cable hanging from the wall. I wrapped my leg around the railing, in case I leaned too far, which saved me from falling but nearly broke my leg. I have splinted it using some old blankets and some of the rope from my supplies. I am nearly out of rope so any cordage I find, I need to collect. I have not examined my leg yet for fear of damaging it more due to lack of light. I will remove the splint and look it over tomorrow as soon as it is bright enough.

I am beginning to lose control of my bodily functions. I nearly urinated all over myself earlier, without warning, while watching for signs of life. I felt a small trickle and realized what was happening. I have tried to keep my waste in the far room but that may not be possible if I go any longer without sleep. Also, I am extremely dehydrated which is taking a major toll on my body. I first noticed it yesterday while urinating, my urine was nearly brown. I have tried to keep from using water as much as possible by moving slowly and straying from doing any hard labor in an attempt to keep my body temperature down. I have decided that I will have to leave this house in about a week if I am going to have any chance of finding food or water before my supply runs out. I regret eating and drinking at a frivolous rate for the first three days, if I would have rationed everything from the start I would have plenty to last an extra week.

I will begin gathering my things and building a packing system tomorrow but I must first get my strength up. I have to find a way to sleep and I will need to eat and drink an extra day's rations the day before I am to leave. I will start planning my escape route tomorrow and begin preparing my exit route. I must find something to help camouflage myself before I leave. If I cannot find something, I may have more problems with the creatures then I want. There is some insulation in the attic and I remember there being some fishing equipment in the basement but getting to the basement may prove to be difficult. I will search, again, for a way to get to the lower floor tomorrow.

Log Entry 5

Yet, another sleepless night. The lack of sleep is really beginning to wear on me. Earlier, I thought I heard someone in the house, a small boy. He kept running through the house, laughing. I tried several times to see who it was but only found shadows. When I yelled out, in hopes of a reply, the creatures outside must have heard me because they have been gathering outside the house. I may not be able to reach the bag at all, now. I have tried to keep quiet since then but it has not seemed to do any good; it is as if they know I am here. I examined my leg earlier; the bruising is immense. I could not bear to touch it, for it was so swollen and sore, even a breeze caused it to throb. I have tried to better stabilize it but I am not able to walk at the moment so I simply crawl. With the aid of a small broken chair, I am able to get to my feet but I must have something to lean against. I feel that if it does not get better within the next day or two, I may die here. I will not allow myself to starve to death or die of dehydration. I think I will just shoot myself after taking out as many of those creatures as possible; saving the last round for myself. I believe I have found a way to get to the lower floor but will not be able to until my leg is more functional. While crawling around, I found a large duct system that may end in the basement. The problem, now, is finding a way to lower myself. I will search for more rope or cordage tomorrow. I did manage to remove the cover of the duct. Looking inside, it seems to go down for about two meters then makes a left turn. I cannot see past the turn so I do not know where, exactly, it leads. Trying to follow it through the wall, I have found that it may lead to the kitchen, but I am not certain. Where I will enter is near the end of the corridor at the top of the stairs.

I examined my escape route again, finding that it will be easy to get to the roof from the opening in the attic if I make it larger. However, getting down the roof to the fence will prove to be difficult, for the roof slopes at an extreme angle on that side. I can only hope that I have the strength to climb down without slipping. So, my final decision is to find something to help me grip the roof better, make the opening in the attic larger, climb over the roof to the opposite side, climb down the roof to the fence, 'tight-walk' the fence, jump to the shed, then jump to the neighboring house's roof, and plan further from there.

Just before nightfall, I found a large piece of glass, from a window, in a closet. I dragged the glass into my living area and broke it, as quietly as possible, into several pieces. I further shaped the pieces, using the hilt of one of my machetes, making them into useful tools. I used a piece to cut up the carpet from the floor and used the carpet to wrap the pieces, forming handles, to keep from cutting myself. Once they were all wrapped, I used some strands of the thread from the carpet, tying it around the wrapped glass, to keep it in place. I think I will be able to use them as knives of some sort, and will fashion some to the ends of sticks for spears later.

I managed to pack almost everything, preparing to leave. I did another inventory check on my equipment. I am estimating that I have about twelve days of food and water left. I think I may be able to break the plumbing under the sink in the bathroom and with some luck, find more water. If I do manage to get to the lower level, I will attempt the same on any of the sinks I find. I can only hope that I can do such without making a lot of noise. I cannot take the chance of attracting more of those creatures.

I need to find a way to draw the creatures away from the house, making my escape much easier. I will attempt to catch a bird or squirrel and break one of its legs or wings and throw it as far as I can. If I cannot manage to do this, I will have to find an alternative. I will have to think about that later; I am much too tired to think clearly. For now, I am going to investigate the loud banging noise coming from down stairs and if everything is fine try to sleep.

Log Entry 6

I, finally, managed to get some sleep, although, it was not by my own freewill. I was rendered unconscious after investigating the noise that was coming from the lower level. I did not see what was causing the noise but if I had to guess it had to be those creatures trying to get in. I could not tell exactly where the noise was coming from but after listening for several moments, I believe it was coming from the kitchen area. I crawled to the bathroom and gathered some broken bits of mirror from the sink. Using a metal hanger, I rigged a security mirror (pole mirror) and reached out as far as I could to see into the kitchen. I nearly had a good view of the kitchen when I suddenly blacked out.

I awoke with my arm dangling from the ledge of the upper floor corridor and the noise continuing. I had no idea what happened nor did I have any head pain. I looked around, finding that it was near dusk again. Quickly, I crawled to the opening in my living area and peered out. I saw a very large group of those creatures. I would have estimated there to be approximately thirty. When I noticed one staring back at me, I ducked, hoping it did not see me and instead was just blindly staring at the house. A moment later, the noise in the lower level ceased.

I began to panic, slightly, when I realized they left my field of view from the opening. Where they went, I do not know. I grabbed my rifle, checked the chamber and magazine, checked for my machetes and drew my bag closer. My throat was dry and I broke into a cold sweat as I waited for them to break through the wall at any moment; nothing. I sat there listening for what seemed to be eternity; nothing. I relaxed a little and drank some water. Then, I recollected myself, rethought the event, and calmed down, telling myself nothing was wrong, even though I knew better. After I had calmed down, I finished the can of beans I had partially eaten yesterday.

Lost in thought for a few moments, I had forgotten about my leg and tried to stand. That may have been the biggest mistake I have made so far. I thought the bone must be fractured because I heard a slight cracking sound and fell back to the ground.

Pulling my pant leg up, I found that the sound did not come from my leg but instead, my boot. I removed my boot to examine it, finding teeth lodged in the sole. At this point pure pandemonium swept over me. I grabbed my rifle quickly and began searching the upper level as quietly as possible. After searching every single crevice I could find, I felt relieved that nothing was present. I returned to my living area, removed the teeth from my boot and examined them. I felt the inside of my mouth, no teeth were missing. I searched around for some answer; nothing. I stared down every wall, every step on the remaining stairs, every opening, and every centimeter of the floor. I then searched what I could see of the lower level; nothing. When I looked up, toward the attic, I noticed a small spot of blood on the edge of the ladder mount.

I slowly climbed the ladder; cautiously watching for any movement. When I reached the top, I found another small spot of blood near the opening in the attic. I stared around and searched every crevice, finding nothing. Once I was convinced nothing was here, I turned back to the opening. I pulled myself up to see outside. Without warning, one of those creatures fell from above me. I reacted instantly, drawing my knife from my side. My heart racing, time seemed to speed up, faster and faster. I swung the blade, sweeping it across the creature's face as it attempted to bite me. I fell backward, trying to kick it out the opening. It jumped in after me, clawing, biting, growling, and screeching as though it were a wild wolverine. I held it away with my right leg, keeping me just out of its reach. I turned my knife to a stabbing position and thrust it into its head. It did not halt. I pulled the knife out and began stabbing at a frantic rate, stabbing it where ever I could. It seemed like hours had passed before it finally fell to the side, lifeless.

I stabbed the lifeless body several more times just to make sure it was dead. I gathered what I could and blocked the opening. I climbed down and closed the attic entrance. I returned to my living area, gathered my things, barricaded the door, and sat in the furthest corner, recounting what just happened. Once I calmed down, I examined myself for any injures. To my relief, my only injury was my leg; none were sustained during the fight. I will not be able to sleep tonight but I know, now, that they are aware of my presence.

Log Entry 7

I did not sleep at all last night. I am still shaken from what happened this morning. I had to repair the opening in the southern most room because those creatures had ripped the barricade from it. Two of them got in, nearly reaching me before I could fire a round. The first took nearly nine rounds before it fell. I was only able to fire one round into the second before my rifle's magazine was emptied. I finished it off with a machete, cleaving all the way through it, causing its left side, from its left ear to its right thigh, to separate from its right side. It reminded me of a scene in a movie. Its blood sprayed all over the room. I quickly cleaned it off; losing another three liters of water, reducing my supply to only a few days. I did not believe I had enough strength to do such; adrenaline is an amazing thing.

As fast as I possibly could, I gathered some equipment and tried to stand again. I nearly fell several times but finally got my balance. I stood still, watching the doorway, until I felt comfortable standing again. I took my first step in three days.

Unstable and weary I began to limp toward the doorway, rifle, reloaded, in hand. Slowly and cautiously, I moved around the bodies lying on the floor. Using a machete, I split their heads, ensuring their deaths.

Once I made it to the doorway, I used military techniques as I rounded corners and searched the upper level, once more. After all was cleared, I moved room to room, searching for their entry-point. I found the southern-most room to be in disarray and the barricade that was over the window, completely destroyed. Hastily, I gathered what I could salvage, obtained more supplies from the other rooms, and rebuilt the barricade. I was nearly finished boarding the window when I heard a loud crash in the lower level.

As though I was racing in a marathon, I ran to the corridor above the stairs. Staring down, I saw several of the creatures roaming, searching, sniffing, tasting, trying to find food. I quietly turned, walking toward my living area and gathered my things with as little noise as possible, watching the doorway the entire time. Once everything was gathered, I strapped my bag to my back, buckling the straps and cinching all of them tightly. With all of my equipment ready, I began to walk toward the attic entrance. I was not going to try to fight my way out.

Holding my breath, I slowly opened the attic hatch and attached the ladder to the mounts. I began to climb, one step at a time, stopping every step to listen. I continuously searched for any signs of movement as I moved toward my destination. Finally, reaching the top, I pulled myself into the attic and caressed the walls and piles of junk with my eyes; nothing. I then slowly moved toward the opening, rifle ready, watching everything around me.

Reaching the opening, I began to remove the boards as quietly as possible. When the first came lose, I set it down carefully near the pool of blood on the floor. That is when I realized the body of the creature I had killed last night was gone. I turned around quickly, finding nothing but an empty room with the exception of a few piles of junk. The opening was pouring light into the attic as though it were being cast from a candle. I calmed myself a little and turned to begin working again.

As I turned around, I smelled it. There in front of me, no more than a few centimeters away, was the mauled face of the creature I thought I had killed last night. Startled, I fell backward, making a loud crashing noise. The creature dived toward me, gnarling, teeth bared. I reacted fast as I held my rifle in front of me. The creature's mouth fell over the barrel as it began biting; as though it were trying to chew through the rifle to get to me. As hard and as fast as I could, I jerked the rifle to one side while turning it, bringing the butt of the rifle toward the creature's head. A loud crunching noise expelled from the creature's mouth as its jaw ripped free from its face. Getting to my feet, I began to smash its head with the butt of the rifle, splattering blood and brain all over the floor.

Once I was sure it was dead, I returned to the opening, I did not care about making noise now, they knew I was there and they were coming.

Log Entry 8

I had to cut my log short last night due to a group of those creatures trying to reach me. I am now sitting on the roof of a building approximately 3 blocks from the house. My left leg (the one I nearly broke) is extremely sore and so is my right foot. It took me nearly the entire night, last night, to make it as far as I did. Traveling like this is extremely difficult and time consuming. I will have to find another means of travel if I am going to make it anywhere before I diminish my supply of water to nothing. For now, I will pick up where I left off last night for sake of accuracy.

I ripped the last board from the window as I heard the creatures climbing the ladder into the attic. Ignoring the massive piece of glass at the base of the window, I climbed out as fast as I could, cutting my foot nearly in half. I did not feel any pain but knew something was wrong. I had no time to deal with it at that moment and ran up the slope of the roof. Once at the top, I fell to my side and slid down the steep slope to the fence. Using my hands to hold the fence, I crouched down and waddled sideways along the fence as though I were a gargoyle scooting across a roof top.

I was nearly to the shed when the creatures reached the beginning of the fence. I moved more hastily as they searched for a way to close the distance between them and me. Looking down, I saw a small group beginning to form at the base of the fence near the shed. I hesitated and then jumped toward the shed. Nearly missing, I caught the edge, holding on as best I could. My feet dangling, I could feel their fingertips brushing the bottoms of my boots as blood poured from my foot onto their hungry, greedy faces.

It took every bit of strength I could muster to pull myself up onto the roof. I sat there for a few minutes gathering my strength. Before I had a chance to recollect myself, the shed began to sway as the structure screeched and cracked. Reacting fast, I jumped to the neighboring house's roof, landing hard on my stomach, knocking the air out of my lungs. It was several moments before I recaptured my breath. I stood and began to run up the slope of the roof toward the house on the opposing side. Sliding down the other side, I reached the fence connecting that house and the neighboring one. I carefully waddled across it as I did the first.

I moved from rooftop to rooftop as quickly and carefully as possible until I reached the house nearest the pharmacy. Because there was not a fence connecting the house to the pharmacy, I had to find another way to cross the alleyway between them. Searching for anything I could use as a bridge, I happened across a very long, large piece of pipe lying in the backyard. Once I spotted it, I had to figure a way to get it from atop the roof. Tearing a coaxial cable free from the wall, I began to throw it toward the backyard as I pulled it loose. Once I had enough to stretch past my target, I retrieved the cable. Using a slipknot and one of the glass knives, I fashioned a jig which would allow me to wriggle the cable under the end of the pipe, using the glass knife for leverage. After several failed attempts, I finally managed to get the cable around the pipe and pulled it tight, carefully. I slowly reeled the cable in, bringing the pipe ever closer with every pull. Once it reached the roof, I grabbed it, not yet freeing the cable. It was longer than I had expected and a bit larger, too. From the roof, the pipe seemed to be approximately six meters long and nearly eight centimeters in diameter.

I pulled it up as far as I needed to, to use the edge of the roof as a pivoting point to swing the other end around into the alleyway. Once the pipe was in the alleyway, I rolled it until it was flush against a dumpster. Pressing down against the end I shoved away from the house's roof with all of my strength. I began to move toward the pharmacy, fast at first and then slowed down, nearly stopping. It felt as though the pipe was going to shift direction, landing me in the middle of the alleyway with those creatures just down the street, heading toward me. It seemed time slowed as I came to a halt and began to panic. But, then, I began to move again, slowly at first but accelerated as I neared the pharmacy.

Hitting the wall, I reached out, catching the roof with my right hand. I pushed down on the pipe as I attempted to pull myself up. I could feel it shifting so I moved quickly. After a hard shove off the wall, I managed to grab the ledge with my left hand. Using my feet, I carefully gripped the pipe, using it to help myself to the rooftop. Letting out a sigh of relief, I fell on to the roof and lay still for several moments.

The pipe crashed to the ground. The ringing, caused by the metal and the asphalt colliding, was significant. I feared that the noise would travel, attracting more creatures to my location. I held my breath as I listened. Nothing seemed to change. The creatures down the street did not seem any more concerned than they were when I was crossing. Relieved, I checked myself over, ensuring that I had not harmed myself any further.

When, I knew, for sure, I had made it in one piece I sat up, examined my surroundings, and then stood. I walked the perimeter of the roof, ensuring myself there was no way the creatures could reach me. I began to feel a harsh throb in my foot and sat down to examine it. My boot was nearly in two pieces with my foot still inside, blood pouring out. I carefully removed my boot to find my foot was only attached by a section approximately four centimeters wide. I used a day's ration of water to clean the wound as best I could. After digging the remaining bits of glass out, I wrapped it tightly, trying to hold it together, with strips of cloth I made by tearing my shirt.

Shirtless, I ate a portion of a can of Spam and drank a small of amount of water. I, then, decided I must find a way into the pharmacy without having to be on the ground. I am too tired now, to do so, so I will instead try to get some sleep and search tomorrow. I will use the tin vent cover on the ventilation shaft to hold a small fire. That should be enough to keep me warm until morning.

Log Entry 9

I slept peacefully last night, whether it is due to massive blood loss or just the lack of nutrition and dehydration, I do not know. I awoke this morning with an intense pain spreading up my leg. When I removed the bandage from my foot, I could already see infection setting in. I knew that I needed to find some type of antiseptic quickly. I re-wrapped my foot and got to my feet. I stood, tenderly, on my foot for a few moments and then began to limp toward the edge of the roof.

Looking down, there was a large group of those creatures gathered at the base of the building. I limped to the opposite side, hoping to see a back exit or a window through which I could access the building. When I approached the edge of the roof, I looked down, finding several more of the creatures. Unfortunately, there were no windows or doors. My foot began to ache more as I walked to the northern side of the building. Reaching the edge, I looked down. To my relief there was a vent which seemed to be just large enough for me to crawl into.

I hastily walked back to my bag, grabbed any rope and cordage I had, and returned to the northern edge of the building. Using double sheet bend knots and double fisherman's knots I tied the rope and cordage together. I secured one end of the makeshift rope to a ventilation shaft and pulled on it as I leaned backward with the rope wrapped around my waist, testing it. Once I felt comfortable, I returned to the northern edge of the building and threw the rope over the side. Searching the ground, I saw no signs of life. I wrapped the rope around my waist and under my right leg, forming a makeshift rappelling rig. Slowly, I lowered myself to the vent. It seemed to be approximately two meters above the ground.

The vent cover was constructed of a thin wire mesh, making it easy to remove. Holding the rope in one hand, I grabbed a loosened edge of the mesh screen and pulled. The vent cover came easily at first but then stopped, leaving an opening too small for me to get through. I set my left foot against the wall and readjusted my grip on the mesh and pulled hard, turning my arm back and forth, trying to loosen the wire more. Finally, after much effort, I managed to rip the mesh free from the duct. I threw the screen upward, landing it on the roof.

I readjusted my grip on the rope, lowered my leg, and grabbed the duct with my free hand. I pulled myself closer to the opening and began to crawl in. Once I was inside far enough, I removed the rope from my waist and began to crawl further into the building. After a period of crawling, I found a vent over-looking the cashier counter. I pried the vent loose, using my machete, causing it to fall to the floor. When it hit the floor, it caused an audible 'clacking' noise. I waited for several moments watching for movement; nothing. Relieved, I slowly lowered myself through the opening, dangling my feet. After a moment, I knew that I had no choice but to let myself fall, risking further injury. I took a deep breath, held it, and let go, bracing myself for impact. As I fell, I quickly let the air out of my lungs, relaxing. I did not realize it, but I was falling toward a shelf. The corner of the shelf clipped my arm, ripping the flesh off my bicep.

I landed hard on my feet, letting out a hoarse grunt of pain. I quickly grabbed my leg, trying to dissipate the pain, to no avail. After a moment of lying there, I bit my lip and stood. Quickly, I walked through the store, searching for antiseptic, pain killers, bandages, water, and food. Finding a small hand basket, I grabbed it and dumped the items in it out. I used the basket to carry the items as I found them. Iodine, Alcohol, ibuprofen, Tylenol, gauze, Ace bandages, tape, and triple antibiotic ointment, but no water. I walked hastily, searching; I found a few cans of food, but no water. I walked toward the front of the store, being careful to stay out of sight of the windows. Then, I spotted it; water. Just outside the door on a display stand, on the opposite side from which the door opened. Disappointed I looked around; there were no creatures in sight. I walked carefully toward the entrance. Once I reached the door, I slowly opened it, scanning outside for any movement. When it was opened approximately quarter-way, I stuck my head out and looked around. No creatures were in sight. I opened the door a little further and attempted to reach around the door to grab a case of the water. I was not able to. I stepped out onto the sidewalk, keeping just inside the door. I tried again; fail. I took another step out, reached again, and managed to grab the edge of the case. Excited, I began to pull the case toward myself, and then looked up toward the northwestern corner of the building. Panicking, because there was a small group of the creatures walking toward me, I jerked the case, ripping the side, causing bottles of water to roll all over the street. I quickly snatched the only two bottles I could and ran inside. I placed the bottles in the basket and ran toward the vent from which I fell. I climbed onto the counter and attempted to reach the vent, but failed. I searched around and noticed the shelf that ripped the flesh from my arm would be tall enough, but was too far away. I set the basket on the counter, walked over to the shelving, and quickly began to shove it toward the vent. Centimeter by centimeter, it neared the opening, slowly. I heard the creatures at the door now, clawing at the glass. I moved faster. As soon as the shelf was close enough, I ran to the counter, grabbed the basket, carelessly spilling it. I moved as quickly as possible, gathering the items and placing them in the basket.

I heard the glass break and stood up. With haste I ran toward the shelving, basket in hand, and began to climb. I could hear the creatures, crushing packages that speckled the floor, as they moved nearer with every step. I pushed the basket into the opening and began to climb in. As I pulled myself up, I felt something brush my foot. Panicking again, I jerked my foot upward, kicking the shelf, causing pain to shoot through my leg. I dragged myself into the vent. Once inside, I grabbed my foot and yelled.

I heard the creatures, trying to climb the shelving and without hesitation, grabbed the basket and began to crawl back to the northern side of the building. The pain and adrenaline made the trip seem long. After what seemed to be hours, I made it to the opening. I could hear the creatures coming and grabbed the rope. I placed the basket handle over my head and wrapped the rope around my waist. I crawled to the edge of the duct and began to climb.

As I climbed, I felt something grab my foot. I did not stop to think and just climb faster while flailing my feet wildly. Eventually, my foot was released as I reached the ledge of the roof. I pulled myself up and over the edge and fell limp. I turned, grabbed the rope and began retrieving it as quickly as possible. I remained there for several moments, recollecting myself and trying to slow my heart. My breathing became ragged as I began to hyperventilate from the over exertion and pain.

Once I calmed myself, I searched through my newly found supplies. I managed to gather a box of gauze, a bottle of iodine tincture, a bottle of isopropyl alcohol, a roll of tape, a tube of triple antibiotic ointment, a bottle of ibuprofen, a bottle of Tylenol, three cans of dog food, two Ace bandages, and a single bottle of water. I searched around me, but did not find the second bottle of water. I must have dropped it when I spilled the basket.

I ate a portion of one of the cans of dog food, drank some water, and cleaned and bandaged my foot and arm. I used the Ace bandages and a piece of the ventilation shaft to construct a makeshift splint for my left leg. Once I felt I had done all I could, I used another piece of the ventilation shaft and some of the wire mesh to repair my boot as best I could. It should hold up for a while, at least until I can find new shoes or repair it properly. I am exhausted and in a lot of pain so I will attempt to sleep.

Log Entry 10

It is nearly daylight now. I did not sleep. My thirst is so great; I can feel my tongue swelling in my mouth. The pain in my foot is intense and it has swollen to nearly the size of a grapefruit. I have not been able to use my left arm due to the massive lesion. My stomach aches as though I were being stomped on. I feel sick, having to refrain from vomiting for fear of further dehydration. I must find a way to get that water in front of the store...

It is near dusk now. I tried several times to get a case of water using what rope and cordage I had and a piece of the ventilation shaft that I fashioned into a makeshift hook. Several times, I had the 'hook' catch the packaging of the case of water but those creatures would investigate the noise and knock the 'hook' loose. I nearly managed to get a case of the water to the roof but approximately two meters from reaching the roof the 'hook' broke, causing the water to crash to the ground, splattering the precious liquid all over the sidewalk.

I attempted again, using a slipknot, leaning over the edge of the roof to compensate for the loss of length due to the knot and loop. Nearly having a case snagged, I leaned too far over the ledge, nearly falling, dropping the rope. Cussing myself for my stupidity, I returned to the northern side of the building hoping to spot something useful. I did not so I moved to the rear of the building, finding a broken ladder and a dumpster near a loading dock. Spawning a plan to reach the ground safely without noise, I returned to my bag.

Searching through the many pockets, I happened across an old, loaded flare gun and a signaling flare. I limped to the front of the store, searching for an opportunity to distract the creatures. After a few moments of observation, I spotted a small car that had been rolled. I aimed the flare gun, carefully, at the broken rear-glass of the vehicle and squeezed the trigger. It took a few moments for the flare to fire, startling me because it was not expected. The flare bounced off the ground and into the vehicle. I waited and watched as the upholstery slowly began to burn.

As I had hoped, the creatures began to wander toward the car. Once I ensured there was none near the building, I returned to my bag, gathered my things and strapped everything down. If I was not able to get back onto the roof, I was not going to leave my equipment. I limped to the rear of the building and examined everything, being cautious. Once I felt confident there were no creatures near the rear of the building, I began to climb down the ladder.

As I stepped on the third rung of the ladder, I heard a popping noise come from the front of the store. I halted for a moment, listening. It sounded as though the car was burning quite well. I began to lower my left foot to the next rung when the car exploded, startling me, causing me to let loose of the ladder, falling onto the dumpster, knocking the air from my lungs. I lied still for a moment, trying to catch my breath. When I heard the creatures coming, I got up quickly and ran around to the northern side of the building. I slowed and began to limp toward the front of the store.

At the corner, I carefully peeked around the building,

searching for signs of movement; nothing. I walked carefully toward the water. Not paying attention, I kicked a glass bottle on the sidewalk. I froze for a moment, listening, hoping they did not hear. When I did not hear anything, I began to move again. It seemed like eternity before I reached the water. I grabbed the nearest case and started toward the police station across the courtyard, which lied on the opposite side of the street. I was becoming excited, thinking I had made it without having to deal with those creatures.

I heard something behind me. I turned my head to look, finding two of the creatures walking toward me. I began to run as fast as I could. Looking behind me, the creatures were gaining and fast. Several thoughts ran through my head as I tried to get away. I did not want to but I thought I would have to drop the water in order to out run them. With every step, they neared. I began to panic, thinking that was the end. Suddenly, I fell; landing hard. Rolling over, eyes closed, expecting the creatures to fall on top of me, I pulled out my knife and began flailing it wildly. When nothing came into contact with my blade, I opened my eyes to find that I had fallen into a sewer and the manhole had only flipped and remained closed. Relieved, I stood, searching around me for the case of water. I could not find it. I assumed that I must have let go of it when I fell, causing it to land outside the manhole.

I waited, sometime, before climbing the ladder to the manhole. Once I reached the top, I slowly lifted the cover and looked around. The creatures were gone but the water was just outside the hole. I slid the cover to one side and climbed out. I walked over and grabbed the case of water. As I stood back up, I heard them coming. I turned to get back to the manhole, spotting them just meters away. I quickly dropped the water into the hole and began to climb down. I was nearly to the bottom when one of the creatures fell in, breaking its leg on impact. The other creature stopped at the edge of the opening and started to growl. I look down; the creature was trying to stand, failing with every attempt. I looked up at the creature at the top, now releasing a loud coughing noise. I pulled my machete from its sheath and climbed to the bottom. Keeping my distance, I swung the heavy blade at the creature's head, cleaving it in two. After a few seconds, it quit moving. I then searched for the case of water. Finding it, I grabbed it and walked along the south tunnel of the sewer. I could still hear the creature at the top coughing.

I began to walk more hastily when I heard more of the creatures making noise. I kept moving until I found a service room. Using my knife I worked the bolt of the door handle loose and pulled the door open. Quietly and cautiously, I entered the room, keeping the door open slightly. Once the room was secured, I closed the door and locked it. I set the water down and dug through my bag, finding my Ferrocerium rod and striker. I gathered what materials I could find by feel that would burn and started a small fire. With the light of the fire I noticed a small pipe in the ceiling which allowed for the sun to shine through, dully.

I enjoyed a bottle of water and ate some more of the dog

food. My foot is so sore now; I may not be able to walk for a couple days. I removed my boot and the bandages to find that my foot had been ripped further. I cleansed the wound as best I could and re-bandaged it. I did the same for my arm. I examined my left leg closely. The bruising is nearly gone and the swelling has gone down. I believe I will stay here for a day or two.

Log Entry 11

Last night was a sleepless one. I could hear the creatures roaming through the sewer tunnels, coughing, growling, and screeching. I wanted it to stop. It seemed as though they knew I was here, but wanted me to think they did not. I tried several times, to no avail, trying to distract myself from the noises. At one point, the creatures even stopped at the door, sniffing loudly, searching. Thankfully, they must not have smelled me, for they continued on.

After extended periods of time, I walked over to the pipe, guessing about what time of day it was. Why I did this, I am not sure. Maybe it was a way to distract myself. Or maybe it was just something of my subconscious mind acting out in an attempt to maintain some form of humanity. I may never know, but what I do know is that if I do not get out of here soon, I may die. My death will be by my own hand, as I will not be able to control my thoughts.

Rolling around on the floor, trying to sleep, I felt as though I was in prison again. Thinking of that, I pulled everything from my bag and off my persons. I laid everything out, using

the flare as a light. Ignorant, I may have been for doing such

but at the time it felt like the right thing to do. Once

everything was laid out, I took an inventory. I had

approximately three meters of fishing line (I used my arm

span to measure it), a large survival knife which was covered

in dried blood, two cans of dog food, one can of tuna,

twenty-two five-hundred milliliter bottles of water,

approximately two-hundred-fifty milliliters of iodine,

approximately four-hundred milliliters of isopropyl alcohol,

four large gauze, approximately half a roll of tape

(approximately fifty meters), a small piece of mesh from the

vent cover, two glass shivs, a small flashlight (without

batteries), two machetes, approximately a meter of parachute

cord, a piece of fine wire approximately thirty centimeters

long, a compass with a cracked lens, a wool blanket (wet and

filthy), a fourth of a tube of triple antibiotic ointment, a

Ferrocerium rod and striker, my notebook, and a pen.

I searched around the room carefully, finding a plastic

clipboard, a paper clip, a small pipe approximately two meters long, a breaker box from which I ripped three pieces of wire approximately one meter long each, and a one-liter glass bottle. I returned to my equipment with the newly found items. Using the wires from the breaker box, I fashioned one of my machetes to the end of the pipe, using a lashing knot. Ensuring it was secure, I tested it by swinging it to and fro; it held. Pleased with my new weapon, I used my knife to cut the machete's sheath into its components, laying them down for me to see all that I had salvaged from it. I pulled the inside strands out of the parachute cord and separated them. I then separated one of the strands into several strands approximately the thickness of thread. I broke a piece of the fine wire off; approximately six centimeters long. I bent the wire in half and wrapped it around itself, creating a primitive needle. I removed my boot and examined my foot. The swelling had gone down slightly. I threaded one of the threads, I made from the parachute cord, through the loop at the bottom of the wire needle. My foot was still too swollen to attempt to stitch it, but when the opportunity arose, I wanted to be able to get it done quickly.

I cleansed the wound with iodine, applied the ointment, and using a piece of the gauze and a piece of the plastic liner from the machete sheath, I wrapped it. Using the cloth from the brim of the sheath I tied the bandage down, snugly. Once my foot was bandaged well, I removed the bandage from my arm. The stench of infection poured from the wound, filling the air around me. I picked the flare up, bringing it close to the wound, and used a glass shiv as a mirror. I could see the yellowish ooze seep from the wound and knew, immediately, it was septic.

I broke the plastic clipboard into two pieces by snapping it parallel to the shorter edges. Using the smooth edge of one of the pieces, I scraped every bit I could out of the wound, gritting my teeth the entire time. After all I could remove was gone, I poured alcohol over the wound and then iodine. I waited for it to dry and applied the ointment. I felt woozy as the flare began to die.

I quickly gathered my things, carefully. In an organized manner I placed the items in my bag, noting where each item was. I then re-bandaged the wound on my arm hastily. I grabbed my boot and bag and dragged them under the pipe which the light had shown through. I sat there and watched as the only light source I had, died, plunging me into darkness.

Log Entry 12

I do not know how long my light source will last as it may go dark outside. Again, I did not sleep. I tried several times but the creatures kept banging and scratching at the door. I was worried the lock would not hold up so I leaned against the door all night. Eventually, they left, I think. I stayed still for a long time before I felt confident enough to move away from the door.

It seemed as though I were locked in a cell; an animal caged and forgotten. Walking through the dark is very dangerous so I sat still most of the time. Every noise incites various ideas as to what could have made the sound. Fear set in when the creatures began to pry at the edges of the door, their fingertips reaching through, their sickening coughing noises just on the other side, their nails breaking off as they scratch at the door as though they were wild animals digging to reach their prey. I am their prey. I am their food. I am their desire. Confused by the silence, I returned to the door, knife in hand. I placed my ear to the door, listening. I heard nothing from the other side of the door, complete silence. I crawled toward the beam of light that began to extend from the ceiling. I sat down under the pipe and removed my boot. Examining my foot, the swelling was nearly gone. I retrieved the wire needle and parachute cord thread from my bag. I retrieved the other medical supplies and placed all of it, neatly, in front of me.

As I removed the bandage from my foot, the skin seemed extremely raw. I poured alcohol over the wound, then the needle and thread. After a few moments, allowing the pain to dissipate, I began to stitch my foot back together. At first, it hurt. It felt as though someone was stabbing my foot with an icepick, then the pain began to fade. Once I reached the side of my foot, I had to take to my knee in order to sew the bottom. Leaning backward, I finished stitching my foot, using one hand.

As I neared the end, something slammed against the door hard. The sound startled me, causing me to rip several stitches out of my foot. In immense pain, I tried to muffle my yelling by placing my arm over my mouth. It did not work, they heard me. They began beating, clawing, and slamming against the door. I quickly turned and began stitching as fast as I could. Once I reached the end, I tied the thread off as best I could with one hand and poured iodine over the suture. I wrapped it in a hurry and replaced my boot. I grabbed my new 'glaive' and crawled toward the door.

I sat against the door for what seemed to be an eternity. The creatures continued to try and gain access but were unsuccessful. After a period of time, they stopped. They began to make noise as though they were fighting and then it went silent. I did not hear anything on the other side of the door. I sat there again, until I felt confident enough to move. The light from the ceiling grew bright and I assumed it was close to noon. I sipped some water and ate the remaining portion of the dog food from yesterday. When I finished the can of dog food, I kept the can. I plan to use it later, if I figure out a way to, to create a primitive fire pot. I assume I will use a mixture of ground charcoal, crushed up mulch (leaves, grass, wood chips, bark, etc.), and some form of fuel.

I think the best way would be to make a paste or putty from the ingredients and pack them into the can tightly. If I can do it correctly, it should make for a decent light source.

After eating, I crawled back to the door. I sat there for some time, listening. There seemed to be nothing, a void, a complete deadness about the world on the other side of the door. I thought about my plan to escape but could not get things to play out right in my mind. Sitting there, I noticed a pain in my head. I investigated the pain with my fingers. I felt a wet spot, but no lesion. Crawling into the light, I investigated further. It was not blood; it seemed to be some form of slime. I stared at it for several moments before I noticed the light dimming, slightly.

I rubbed the substance between my fingers and noticed it had the same consistency as the membrane that covers the meat of a freshly skinned animal. I felt the spot, finding more. I began to pull the material from my head, hair with it. There seemed to be so much of it. It seemed like I dug at the spot for hours. Finally, I felt something hard and tapped it. I do not know what the stuff was, but my head is extremely sore now. I will have to wait until I have a mirror to see what is causing the pain. For now, my light is growing dim and I must sleep.

Log Entry 13

It is about midday. I did not sleep last night. This time the creatures did not make noise; it was dead silent. Even with the silence, I could not sleep; I could not bring myself to lie down. I sat under the pipe almost the entire night, scratching. I itched so badly. I did not know why but I could feel 'bugs' crawling on me. I saw them, in the dark, their little beady eyes staring back as they crawled across the floor. I tried several times to catch them, only to fail.

It is nearly dark outside. I sat my notebook down to investigate, what I thought was, someone whispering on the other side of the door. I crawled to the door and sat down, pressing my ear against it. The cool steel felt so good against my skin and then I was waking up. Sweating profusely, I crawled back to the pipe. I sat there, confused, mind racing, and ate the can of tuna and drank some water. I feel as though I am dying, or am I just going insane? I do not know. I need to get out of here and soon.

Tonight, I will try to sleep. At the first sign of light from the pipe, I will attempt to escape. I cannot stay here any longer, I must move on. I have one can of dog food left and approximately nineteen bottles of water. I feel I have plenty of water but I need food soon. I have gathered my things in preparation. I think my best option would be to wait until there is no sound outside the door, unlock it quietly, open it cautiously, peek around, and try to sneak out. If I can make it to another manhole further in the sewer, I may be able to get out without having to fight any of those creatures. I am not going to get my hopes up though.

By morning I should be able to walk. My foot is beginning to feel better but I know that it will not heal properly, or at least decently, if I do not stop walking on it. I must find a place where I will have plenty of food and water for a couple weeks and will not have to worry about those creatures getting in; or at least where I will be able to hold them off without much of a struggle. I do not know where I will go or how I will get there, but I think I will head south. I believe if my memory serves correct, there is a military base approximately seventy kilometers (by road) southeast of here. I do not know if that is true, but it is worth a try. I do not know what I will find; if it is there.

The trip to the base, that may or may not exist, is going to be a long and brutal one. I cannot simply walk down the street or highway to it. I must take a more covert route in order to avoid those creatures. It would be much easier to navigate my way there if I had a map. The nearest shop to get a map would be the general store near the mall. I do not know how far it is from where I am, nor do I know how to get there from where I am without following the streets. However, if I do make it there, I should be able to find a map and, if I'm lucky, food.

I may also be able to get into the mall. If I am able to, it may be possible to find a gun and some ammo. I have lost my .22 rifle somewhere; I did not notice it until earlier. I had not thought about it, but I have not had it since the pharmacy. I do not know if I left it behind in my haste or if it fell off my back when I fell, or if I lost it, in the sewer. I have not found it, roaming around this room, so I had to have lost it before I entered. I only had one magazine of rounds left (ten), so it would not have been much good. I need to find a larger caliber firearm, but I must maintain a light load. I will try carrying any ammo I can find, which ever seems best, I will attempt to find a firearm to match.

The back of my head is extremely sore. I investigated the pain with my fingers, finding a spot where the skin had been ripped from the skull. I tapped on the hard spot I felt. When I heard the unmistakable sound of something thumping bone, I knew my skull was bare. I cleansed the wound and wrapped it. I have no idea how the injury happened. I only hope it is not too severe. I will wait until I find a mirror or something reflective to see how bad it really is. The light is becoming too dim to see now. I believe I will sit here for a while and then try to sleep. I have a hard journey to begin tomorrow.

Log Entry 14

Finally, the time had arrived to escape. I sat there preparing myself for several moments. Once I felt I had the strength, I stood. At first I could not walk; it took me a few moments to gain my balance. As soon as I was able to, I began walking toward the entrance. At the door, I stopped, pressing my ear to the steel, listening. I heard nothing, deadness, a silence that sends chills down the spine. I waited for a few moments, listening carefully.

With my glaive ready, I unlocked the door so slowly that it felt as though it took hours to turn the lock completely. I, then, opened the door as slow as one would defuse a bomb. Once the opening was large enough for me to look out, I slowly pressed my head forward. The darkness of the tunnel was no different than that of the room; impossible to see in. I stood there, listening for the slightest of sounds. I did not hear any creatures roam; only water dripping.

I stepped out of the room, feeling with my left foot. Once I felt the floor was safe and clear, I stepped further out. I slid foot after foot, carefully, across the floor as I slowly moved forward. With every step, I stopped and listened for any movement, any sound that would alarm me.

Suddenly, I felt something in front of me. I squatted down, carefully placing my hand on it. I caressed the object cautiously, ready to retreat at any moment. With my fingers brushing the surface of the item, I could feel clothing, tattered and wet. I continued to move my hand along the body of the object; a dip, then flesh. I could feel skin beneath my fingertips, coarse and yet wet. Caressing further, I found a large hole; further investigation implied it was a horrid bite wound. Feeling further, I found *its* face. The jaw had been removed.

Startled, I jumped to my feet. I stood there for a few moments, listening. I heard nothing and began to move around the body. Again, slowly, I moved forward. After just a few small steps, I felt something in front of me again. I squatted down, once more. I, cautiously, laid my hand upon the object. It felt as though it were a pile of organs. I felt around, searching for more clues. My fingers brushed

something soft, yet firm, and wet. I explored further, finding

that it was another body; this one sundered at the waist.

I quickly stood. As I started around the body, I heard

something. Stopping and holding my breath, I listened

carefully. It seemed to be some kind of rodent. I listened,

paying close attention to which direction the sound was

coming from. Once I thought I knew where the animal was

hiding, I started in that direction. Getting excited at the

thought of food, I did not think to navigate the tunnel

carefully.

Tripping over another body, I fell to the floor. The sewage

seemed to be approximately six centimeters deep, covering

my hands. I stood again and attempted to clean my hands off

on my pants. After wiping what I could off, I started down

the tunnel once more, heading southward. I paid close

attention to the placement of my feet as I walked deeper into

the tunnel.

Holding my glaive, as though a ringmaster would hold a

chair when fighting back a lion, I moved slowly around a bend in the tunnel. I could see light shine against the wall, dimly. Continuing on, stopping and listening with every step, I finally reached a point where I was able to see down the tunnel to the source of the light.

I could see a large opening at the end of the tunnel, a lake of water just on the other side. I began to walk faster, excited at the thought of freedom. As I neared the opening, I saw several bodies lying scattered. The light shining upon there bloody bodies, the image burned into my memory. It looked like a picture one would find in a documentary about Hitler's reign.

I stopped to examine the bodies. Each was riddled with holes; so many that some of the bodies were no longer recognizable as human. Their entrails, bits of bone, blood, and chunks of flesh scattered as though it were confetti. Their skulls crushed; their limbs mutilated and strewn; their bodies piled as though it were done in haste.

Despite the carnage, none of them seemed to have any

definite bite wounds. When I finally recovered from my shock and took a breath, the smell overwhelmed me. The bodies must have been decomposing for some time. If I had to guess, I would say from the start of the outbreak.

They had nothing of use on them so I said a prayer and moved on. Reaching the edge of the opening, there was a sloping concrete slab, leading down to a sewage facility. I sat down and began to scoot down the slope. The concrete was rough, ripping the rear of my pants. Despite this, I continued to slide down the slope as far as I could. Once I reached a level area, I stood up and walked along the edge of the large pool of sewage.

I walked until I reached the corner of the pool, leading me to a ledge. Looking down, I estimated it to be approximately four meters to the ground. I turned to the right to continue on the ledge, walking toward the facility. I nearly lost my balance several times, almost falling into the pool.

When I reached the facility, I walked around the outside, searching for a way to get to the roof. I wandered nearly the entire perimeter of the building before I found a small fire escape ladder. I slid my glaive into a loop of the webbing on the outside of my bag, retrieved my knife and began to climb. When I reached the top of the ladder, I peeked over the edge of the roof. Seeing nothing but ventilation units, I climbed the rest of the way up. Once at the top, I replaced my knife and grabbed my glaive. Ready for a fight, I began searching the roof. I took small steps, stopping with every step to listen as I did in the sewer.

Walking around one of the large ventilation units, I spotted a table with boxes next to it and a HAM radio on top of it. I stopped. Looking around, I did not see anyone; nor did I hear anyone. I waited for what seemed to be hours before continuing on.

Slowly, I walked toward the table, watching around me, for signs of movement. Once I reached the table, I looked in the distance over the table. I did not see anything in the field that lay before the building and turned around. I searched the rest of the roof. When I found the roof access door, I checked to make sure it was secure. I then returned to the table and examined the boxes.

Opening one of the boxes, I found several M.R.E.'s. Opening the second box, I found several cans of food and some bottles of water. In the third box, there were various medical supplies but nothing more than what one would find in a first aid kit. The fourth box contained what seemed to be various firearm components. The fifth and final box had three four-liter jugs of water wrapped in a plastic film.

I sat down, enjoyed an M.R.E. and helped myself to a couple bottles of water. After eating, I removed my boots. The sewage had seeped in causing my feet to become raw. I quickly removed the bandage from my foot and cleansed the wound thoroughly, leaving it to dry. I then removed the bandage from my arm and cleansed the lesion. Once my foot had dried, I applied the last of the ointment I had and wrapped it with a new bandage. I examined my arm as best I could and decided that I only needed to cover it. I removed a piece of one of the cardboard boxes and taped it to my arm. I then washed my boots out and left them to dry.

I tried to turn the radio on but no luck; the batteries were dead. I searched around looking for a replacement but there were none to be found. I moved the boxes from the edges of the table. Feeling weary, I crawled under the table and lay down. Writing this entry has drained what energy I had, so now I am going to sleep.

Log Entry 15

I found a man lying under my table when I returned last night. I have him chained to the access door. Having him there will give me a little more time to get away if anything tries to come up the stairs from inside the building. I am waiting for him to awaken so that I may question him. For now, I am writing in his journal *for him*.

He seems to be a bit crazy. I have concluded, at least from reading his journal that he has been out there for about two weeks. In one of his entries, he writes about tearing the flesh from his own head and then in another, he finds the wound and does not know how it was sustained. After reading his journal, I examined his head. The wound looked self-inflicted and his skull is bare, however, I cannot be sure; it may be a bite.

When he wakes up, I will examine him, to make sure he has not been infected. He looks rough and is quite pale. I am curious as to where he came from and how he has made it thus far. He seems to have a badly injured arm and the boot on his right foot is falling apart. He is shirtless and seems to shiver a lot. I cannot tell if he is cold or just twitching. I do not know who he is or *how* he is. I have no clue if he is insane or just scared. I will find out when he awakes.

That motherfucker has me chained up to a damn door! And he wrote in my book. My book! I cannot believe this. I knew it was too good to be true. At least he let me have my notebook back. I cussed him for writing in it. He invaded my privacy! He walked away after handing it to me and said he will return when I calm down.

It seemed like hours before he returned. I tried, the entire time, to get this damn chain off my ankle. If it was not for my bad foot, I may have been able to get out of it. When he did come back, he brought me a bottle of water and asked me what my name was. I just stared at him with a pissed off look on my face. He eventually said, "Fine, I'll let you sit there until you decide to talk. Remember, the quicker I get to know you the quicker that chain falls off." He walked away as though I were just a dog chained up in the yard.

The guy seems like he is nice, or at least considerate, but I cannot let my guard down. He looks to be approximately two meters tall, he is quite large. He has broad shoulders and is, over all, a big guy. His hair looks black, but I cannot tell for sure. He has a certain 'coldness' about his eyes as though he is 'heartless.' I do not know his name but what I do know is that he seems to know what he is doing and takes no chances when dealing with people.

He returned after a period of time and simply stared at me. I stared back, neither of us saying anything. It felt like an eternity and I finally gave in. I said, "Alright! What?! What do you want?!" He turned to walk away as I said "What?" He just looked over his shoulder and said with an absolutely straight face, "Are you done yelling?" I looked back at him and replied, "What is it you want?" After a long moment of silence, he asked, "Where did you come from?" I told him about the house. He looked intrigued. "You're a moron," he said. I became angered by his remark.

He stood there for a moment and then asked, "Who are you?"

I simply stared back at him. "What is your name?" I replied, "That's not important." With a witty attitude, he responded, "Alright, That's-not-important, how did you make it this far without any help? You don't look like the type that's cut out for this kinda stuff." I just stared at him and replied, "I know you read my logs, you said so yourself. That should be good enough."

After a few awkward moments of silence, he looked at me and asked, "Why?" I looked back at him confused, asking, "What do you mean 'why?'" He pointed at my book and said, "You write everything you do. Why?" I grabbed my book, slowly, and stared at the cover, deep in thought for a few moments. I did not look at him when I said, "Because, I hope that it will keep someone from making the same mistakes I did." He just looked at me with a strange look upon his face; a mix of confusion and curiosity. He simply replied, "I don't understand." I asked him, "Are you a caveman or something?" He remained silent and walked away.

I sat here until it was near dusk before he returned. He approached me and asked about the wound on the back of my head. I explained to him that I did not know how it came to be. He told me about my logs and my first account of the wound. I told him he read it wrong or he was crazy because I never wrote such. He told me to turn to the page so I did. I read the entire entry and when I looked up he was gone. Confused by the entry, I sat here thinking about everything. I do not remember writing that entry nor do I remember peeling pieces of flesh from my skull.

It is getting too dark to write and I must pay attention to everything around me. I do not know what he will try if I go to sleep so I must find something to help me stay awake. I guess I will try to escape. This may be my last entry so for those who find this: Keep moving and do not trust anyone.

Log Entry 16

He has not killed me, yet. I am still chained to the roof access
door and have not eaten since the night he chained me up
(while I was sleeping). He has brought me water every six to
eight hours though. When I asked him about food, he simply
stared at me and said, "The rule of three," and walked away.
What he meant by that I have yet to figure out. Maybe he will
tell me at a later time, if I ask.

It rained today. He brought a tarp over to me and threw it
over the edge of the roof access and me. He did not say
anything when he did it, acting as though he was just taking
care of an abandoned dog for the time being. I want him to
let me free. I do not know what he plans nor do I know how
long he is going to keep me. I have tried to pry any answers I
can from him but have had no luck. He is like a stone; he
seems to have no emotions; the inability to sympathize; a
void where is heart (or soul) should be. He acts like an
extremely intelligent and functional robot or cyborg.

After it quit raining, the man brought a shotgun when he

came over to me. He leaned it against the ventilation unit in front of the access door and walked to my position. He stared at me lying on the ground, weak, unable to fight and knelt down. He grabbed my face with his right hand as though I were a snake and he was trying to avoid being bitten. He stared into my eyes peeling them open one by one with is left hand. He blew, into each eye, a quick puff of air. When I blinked rapidly but had no other reaction, he stood up.

Looking up, I saw him digging in his pocket. When he pulled his hand out, he dropped a single shotgun shell in front of me and walked away.

I lay there, staring at the shell for several moments. Then, I looked at the shotgun and sat up. I stretched as far as I could, trying to reach the shotgun, but failed. After several attempts, I stopped and looked around me. I crawled back to the door and grabbed the tarp. Carefully, I pulled it down, trying not to make noise while doing so. Once I had the tarp, I twisted it up, like one would a towel when wringing it out, and stretched out as far as I could again. Throwing one end of the tarp while holding the other, I attempted several times before I managed to get it around the shotgun. As carefully as I could, I slowly pulled the tarp, bring the butt of the shotgun closer with every tug. Finally, the shotgun fell, but just out of my reach.

It took several more attempts to get the shotgun close enough to grab. Once I was able to reach it, I pulled it to me as though it were my own child, lost in this world. I quickly opened the action and grabbed the shotgun shell. I tried to load the gun but the shell would not fit. I examined the chamber and the shell, closed the action and reopened it, then tried again. The shell would not fit. I looked at the base of the shell, it read: Winchester 12 ga. I then looked at the shotgun: Remington 20 ga. Annoyed and confused, I sat the gun down and crawled back to the door.

I pondered the puzzle of the gun and the shell for some time. Why would he leave a shell that did not fit? Why would he leave the gun to begin with? What is he doing? Is he testing me? My train of thought continued until approximately midday. I sat there sipping on my water staring at the gun until he finally returned.

He walked to the shotgun, bent down and picked it up.

Without saying a word, he turned and walked away. He did not look at me nor did he act disappointed. I sat there quietly for a while and he eventually came back. This time he brought food. I was pleased with the idea of getting to eat. But I was torn. What if he poisoned it? Why would he poison it? Why is he feeding me if he does not want me alive? Why would he not just shoot me? I was cautious about eating the food. He stood nearby watching me the entire time I ate. When I finished (approximately an hour or so later), he put his hand out as though he wanted something from me. I stared at his hand, confused. He squatted down and looked at me with a straight face. After a few moments of awkward silence, he spoke, "Have you been bitten, scratched; contaminated in any way?" I just stared at him. He reached behind him and pulled out a large knife. He stared at me for a moment holding the knife in his right hand with his left wrapped around it, loosely, while he squatted. I replied after a short moment, "No, not that I know of."

He looked at my foot and asked, "How?" I looked at my foot and replied, "A window, trying to get out of the house." He touched the back of his head and asked, "How?" I felt the back of my head and said, "I don't know. I woke up like this. I read my logs and it doesn't make sense. I have no idea why I wouldn't remember such a thing." He looked at me for a moment as though I were stupid and then said, "In your 'logs' you found a room in the sewers. How long were you there before you wrote the first 'log' about your head?" I looked at him, thinking, and said, "I don't know, a couple days." He stood and walked away.

It was nearly dark before he returned. When he came back, he knelt down in front of me. He looked at me and asked, "How do you feel?" I looked at him as though it were a redundant question. He said, "I know you feel like shit, but do you feel anything weird or funny?" I looked at him confused and said, "No." He paused for a moment and stated,

"You try anything and you're dead. You act funny and you're dead. You touch me and you're dead. Do I make myself clear?" I sat quietly for a moment and then replied, "Crystal." He grabbed the padlock on the chain and said, "Good."

He unlocked the padlock, removed the chain from my ankle, chained the door closed and walked away. I laid there for some time. He came back a few moments later with a bottle of water and some medical supplies. He set them down in front of me. He started to walk away again and said, "When you're ready, there's a chair over here," and disappeared behind a ventilation unit. I hastily cleansed my wounds and bandaged them as best I could. When I finished, I tried to stand but was too weak. I fell to the ground and began to crawl.

When I finally reached the table, I had found when I first arrived; he was sitting in a chair next to an empty one. I crawled over to the empty chair, grabbed the back and pulled myself up. I slid my feet one by one to stand next to the chair and fell into it. He looked at me and grinned, "Feeling weak?" I just stared at him. He reached down, grabbed something and threw it at me. I caught it, somewhat. I looked at it for a moment then looked back at him. He said, "If you don't want it, I'll just keep it." I looked back at the package. I slowly opened it, afraid of what may be inside. When I pulled the flap on the large envelope open, I peeked inside. I reached in and found a sweatshirt. Quickly, I pulled it out and put it on.

He looked at me and said, "Food's in that box," pointing at the box next to me, "water in that box," pointing at the box on the other side of him, "medical in that box," pointing to the box under the table; "ration it." I looked back at him and asked, "Who are you?" He looked back at me and, with a straight face, said, "I can be your best friend or your worst nightmare. Either way, you may call me: 'Sukata.'" I nodded my head and said, "You can call me: 'Kmoneiethe'" (pronounced Monith). He nodded in acknowledgement and offered me a bottle of water. I took it and began writing in my book.

It is becoming too dark to write now and Sukata said we cannot use candles, for they are attracted to light.

Log Entry 17

Sukata was gone when I awoke this morning. I searched around for any signs of him or his body. I do not know where he went but hopefully he is back soon. He took all of my weapons with the exception of my knife. He, either, has them hidden or with him. I do not know if he has left me for dead or is just out looking for supplies. He left a single bottle of water and an M.R.E. on the table. The boxes and the radio were gone, also.

I have no idea where I am nor do I have anyway of figuring it out without leaving the safety of the roof. I dare not roam near the edge, for I have seen several eyes staring back at me and at one point saw a light off in the distance. I thought about yelling toward the light but did not. I was not sure who or what it was and did not want to attract unwanted attention to myself.

This M.R.E. is the only food I have. It may be the only food I have until I find more, unless Sukata returns. I knew that I should not have trusted him. I cannot give up my hopes just yet though. He may return but I will ration everything as he may not, leaving me on my own again. He does not seem like the kind of guy to put someone in such a position but he does seem like the type to leave you for dead if he needed…or just simply wanted…to.

It was nearly midday before I awoke. I do not remember going to sleep last night. Sukata and I had spent some time talking. Well, I did a lot of the talking and he just asked questions. After I would answer a few questions, he would look at me as though he had discovered something and then ask a few more. It seemed as though he were prying information from me without me knowing, but how? He would ask strange things like: "What's your favorite animal?" or "What's your take on birds?" I do not understand why someone would ask such questions, but that is what he wanted to know.

I believe Sukata may be a little mad. He stared at the radio last night as though he were trying to power it with his mind or something. I do not know what he was thinking or what he saw but he did act quite strange. At one point in the night he began to yell obscenities at the creatures in the woods. I did not understand what he was saying; it was all gibberish to me. He would also say strange things to me as though I were supposed to respond in a comprehensive way. When I just stared at him, he would chuckle slightly and then wander off somewhere.

I even thought he was going to kill me, during one of our conversations. I do not remember what I said but he turned and stared at me with an evil look on his face. After a few moments of me trying to talk my way out of the situation, he simply laughed and said, "I'm just fucking with ya." He seems to have a very twisted and sick sense of humor about him.

It is hard to tell when Sukata is joking or being serious. He has a strange way of going about things. I guess it will just take some time to get used to it and understand it. He never really talks about his past nor does he talk about his family, if he had or has one, or even where he came from. He, more or less, has a hole where most people have emotions. I do not understand how someone can be so cold about everything. It has been quite a long day. I have tried several different things to occupy myself. I have even tried to write about Sukata but there just is not much to go off of right now. I have yet to get a good look at him because it was either raining, he was covered with something, or it was too dark to see. I have searched nearly every centimeter of this roof, finding nothing of use. I have not been this bored since I came to America some eight years ago. It reminds me of being in the airport all over again.

I do like this situation better than the room in the sewers. I am able to get away if need be, I have light, I can see everything around me, I do not feel as though I am in prison again, and I do not have to worry about the creatures smelling me out. I also am able to treat my wounds better and can see improvement in them already. My arm should be healed within the week and my foot shortly after that. I would estimate it to be a three week recovery to full functionality. That worries me though, because I do not have any source of food or water.

I found the medical supplies. They were not hidden; Sukata had set them atop one of the ventilation units. I assume he did so to ensure they did not get ruined if those creatures got up here. I would imagine that if he did not want me to find them he would have hidden them better, as he did the food and water. I find it strange that he would leave this, unless he did intend on returning.

Searching through the medical supplies, I found a large piece of rolled up butcher's paper. Unrolling it, I realized it was actually a hand drawn map of the town. Sukata is a very intelligent man, for he took great care to mark, label, and detail everything. He even went as far as to put indicators on areas he had explored, illustrating the level of danger in each. I am assuming that the pencil marks indicate a low-danger area, a pen mark indicates mid-danger area, and marker indicates high-danger area. However, after examining it more closely, I realized that these marks were not for the danger of the area. He had used various colors of highlighter to indicate danger. The pencil, pen, and marker indicated something else, something significant.

I shall ask him, when he returns; if he returns, what the map reads. I do not understand his system completely but he seems to have something figured out. It is getting late and there is a group of those creatures coming toward the building. They are quite a ways away for now but I need to get something to help me fend them off if they continue toward me. I shall continue my logs as soon as possible.

Log Entry 18

This is the second day Sukata has been missing. I have not seen any sign of him nor have I heard anything. I have searched the field in front of the building and the woods on the southern end of the building. I have seen several of those creatures but no sign of life otherwise.

It rained again earlier. I used the table as shelter until it passed. It seemed to rain for hours. When it first started, I searched the roof for anything to catch the rain but had no luck. I eventually huddled under the table and waited it out. At one point, during the storm, I thought I heard Sukata coming up the ladder at the rear of the building, but when I investigated it, it was just the rain hitting a sheet of metal leaning against the wall. When I realized what it was, I returned to the table and stayed there. I did not move again until the rain let up.

Once the rain gave in, I crawled out from under the table, grabbed the map, and wandered the roof. I checked everything I could; pried open vents, opened ventilation units, even checked cracks in the walls. I did not find anything of use. I, then, returned to the table, wiped away as much water as possible from the table and chair, and sat down. I waited a few minutes and then pulled the map out. I unrolled the map and began to study it carefully. I tried hard to figure out the puzzle. I could not figure what I was missing. I thought about everything, taking all aspects of the map into consideration. Eventually, I stopped trying, thinking there was a piece of the puzzle missing. That is when it hit me. There is a piece of the puzzle missing!

Sukata must have the piece I need with him. I do not know if it is a bit of information or if it is another piece of the map or special compass or if I am just crazy and could not figure out the puzzle. So, to ensure that I am not crazy, I viewed the map over from every angle. After staring at it until it was becoming dusk, I decided I could not solve the puzzle.

Sukata is just too smart or mad.

I have rationed the M.R.E. and water out, separating it into a five day supply. I believe that if I take it easy, and watch my activity, that should last me until Sukata returns or I decide to leave. I think that if Sukata is not back by tomorrow, I may start planning my route to the general store and mall. Hopefully Sukata's map is accurate enough for me to figure out a safe path.

The creatures below seem to come closer and closer to the building searching for food. I can only hope that they do not find me or find a way up here. I keep an eye on the ladder and access door but if they wanted to, they could overtake me in a matter of seconds, considering I only have a survival knife.

For now, I will eat, drink, and sleep. When I awake, I hope to see Sukata has returned, for I do not want to remain here alone without protection for much longer. I do not know how long I can hide out here. I am too weak to leave due to the lack of food and water but I may have to anyway.

Log Entry 19

Still no sign of Sukata. I am beginning to think he left me for dead. I do not know how much longer I can wait here. If he is not back by tomorrow night, I am leaving the next morning at first light. That will give me enough time to check my plan over and get myself prepared. This is going to be a long and hard journey, for I am weak and my foot has not yet healed. My plan, for now, is to get to the ground, cross the field, get onto the highway overpass, get to the other side of the interstate, walk down about a kilometer or so, then follow the train tracks over to the train station. From there I will simply walk across the street to the general store and then use the alleyways to get to the mall. If I do all of this carefully, I should be able to make it without having to fight.

After searching around today, I found a small opening between the building and the sewage tanks. If I am not mistaken, there is a ladder from the catwalk atop the sewage tanks to the ground. I believe I will use the ladder on the side of the building to get down, make a run for the sewage tanks, and climb the ladder to the catwalk. Doing so will allow me to gain access to the observation tower in the center of the sewage facility. If I can reach the tower, I may be able to find something of use.

That was a close call. I got to the tower without any problems. But when I opened the door, three rotting bodies fell out. All three of them had been shot in the head, one through the inside of the mouth (as though by suicide). From the way they fell out, it seemed as though they were trying to hold the door shut, but there were no scratches nor teeth marks on the outside of the door...strange.

Once I searched all of the bodies, trying to keep from vomiting, I dragged them out onto the catwalk and closed the door, locking it behind me. The stench from the bodies was strong and lingered. Covering my face with the sweater Sukata gave me, I climbed the stairs to the observation deck of the tower. I set all of the items that I collected from the bodies on the small card table setting just inside the railing and began searching everything. Within a matter of minutes, the stench began to seep through the sweater.

After several hours of searching, placing everything I found on the card table, I returned to the table to examine my finds. Altogether, I found a nine millimeter pistol with three rounds of ammunition, an extra magazine (empty), a large pocket knife, a utility knife with a broken blade, a coffee mug (I am estimating it to be approximately three-hundred milliliters in volume), a small flashlight with dead batteries, a cigarette lighter that still has a small amount of fuel remaining (judging by the size of the flame), a half-liter bottle about half-full of water, a clipboard (large, metal, and box-like), three ink pens, a small desktop fan, and a belt. Gathering all of my new items, I started down the stairs.

As I neared the door, I could hear the unmistakable coughing noise those creatures make. I quickly halted, turned around, and climbed back up the stairs. When I reached the top, I set everything on the table again and picked up the pistol. I chambered a round and took the safety off. I then pulled out my knife and prepared myself for a fight.

After what seemed to be an eternity, nothing happened, so I tried to see where the creatures were through the observation window. It took several attempts to find a section of the window that would allow me to see the area in front of the door clearly. Kneeling on one of the control panels, I leaned against the glass. I could see four of the creatures devouring the rotting bodies I found.

I sat down on the control panel, wondering how I was going to get out of the situation. I sat there for several minutes before I decided to search the tower for another way out. Tired and hungry, I looked everywhere I could without making noise. I checked every crevice I came across and anything that looked like a door or hatch. I searched until it was near dusk and having not found anything, I gave up. I decided this was going to be my new tomb.

I left what remained of the M.R.E. on the roof, thinking I would return quickly. I had only brought my water and knife with me. I know, after searching, that there is no food of any sort in this tower. If I have to I will shoot myself before I starve to death. The idea of starving is a painful one.

When I realized Sukata would not know where I was if he did return, I used my knife to cut the index finger on my left hand and tried to write on the window facing the building. Due to being dehydrated, my blood would not flow freely, so I had to cut my left hand. Cutting it deeply, the blood began to flow. I cupped my hand to hold the blood as it pooled. Using the index and middle fingers on my right hand, I wrote on the window, in large and bold letters: "HELP." I did not remember to write the letters backwards, so the word will read backwards when looking at it from the outside.

It is getting dark and my light is fading. I will not sleep tonight. Instead, I will be watching the door carefully. Hopefully, though I am not going to count on it, Sukata returns by morning and sees that I am gone. Then, I can only hope that he sees the "HELP" in the window and he comes to find me.

Log Entry 20

It was a long night. Those creatures did not try to get in but I knew that they could try at any moment. I sat at the top of the stairs holding the pistol and my knife, ready to fight at the first sign of movement. The agony and irony of the situation became too much to handle. I could not take it much longer and decided to write to pass the time.

Judging by the position of the sun, it is approximately midday. I have not seen, nor heard, any sign of Sukata. I have awaited his arrival for some time now. I believe it has been four days since the last I saw him. I hope he comes soon. I am nearly out of water; I may have enough to make it through another day; and I have not eaten in two days.

The creatures have not moved since earlier today. I have no idea how much longer they can eat on those bodies. They have strewn the intestines and other organs about as though they were using them to decorate the catwalk. From what I am able to see, they had thrown intestines over the railing and smashed some of the organs into the catwalk. Some of the bones on the bodies are bare, the flesh completely stripped from them. The faces of the bodies are entirely mutilated; the eyes missing, the jaws nearly or completely torn off, the noses either missing or hanging by a small strip of flesh, and some of the ears have been chewed apart.

I can only imagine what my fate would be, given those creatures get to me before I am able to commit suicide. I fear I may not be strong enough to go through with shooting myself. I would like to think that I would be brave enough to finish it before I am devoured but I will not know until the time comes. To avoid the situation altogether, I am going to continue my search for another way out.

It is near dusk now. The creatures are beating on the door. The noise is pounding in my skull or is that my heart? I cannot tell. I am sweating profusely, losing water fast. I can feel my hands clamming up. I am worried about what will happen if they get in. I cannot see the creatures through the window, only increasing my anxiety. I have no idea what they are doing.

The noise seems to be getting louder, closer almost. I think I am going mad; it has been nearly an hour since it started. I cannot hear anything but the sound of something pounding against the metal door. My head feels as though someone has taken a large hammer and began smashing it. I fear I may not be able to take much more of the noise. If the noise continues for much longer, I will not live long enough to see what happens.

It is night now, I am writing using a lantern Sukata had brought back with him. I will recount what happened in the tower.

I checked the pistol to make sure a round was chambered. I turned the pistol, inserting it into my mouth aiming upward toward my cranium. I squeezed the trigger, but nothing happened. I pulled the pistol from my mouth and turned it in my hands, examining it. I pulled the slide back, loading another round into the chamber, ejecting the initial round onto the floor. I reinserted the pistol into my mouth and squeezed the trigger again.

Frustrated and the pounding noise getting louder, I pulled the pistol from my mouth and examined it again. I realized what the issue was and adjusted the safety switch. I inserted the pistol into mouth again. I squeezed the trigger, but again, nothing happened. I removed the pistol becoming quite angry. Shaking with anger, I turned the pistol, flipped the safety switch and pulled the slide back to make sure it moved freely, loading the final round into the chamber and ejecting the other to the floor.

As I inserted the pistol into my mouth for the final time, I heard the door burst open. I could hear footsteps moving hastily up the stairs. I clenched my eyes shut and began slowly squeezing the trigger as tears began to roll down my cheeks. Before the pistol could fire, I heard Sukata ask, "What the hell are you doing?" I opened my eyes and released the trigger, happy to see him standing there.

He looked at me as though I were completely moronic for even taking such an action into consideration. I lowered the pistol to the floor and looked up at him. As he stood in the dim light from the window, I could see him clearly. He was a large Native American, almost Mexican-looking, man with one of my machetes, bloody, in his right hand, the head of one of the creatures in the other. He was slouched over slightly with his head tilted to his left as he stared back at me. I sat there quietly for a moment before I replied, "I was going to shoot myself. I saw what those creatures did to those bodies out there. I saw what they did. I was not going to die like that. I…I…" I broke out into tears, planting my face in my hands. He just stood there, then turned and began to walk out of the tower. I quickly asked, "Where are you going?" He just mumbled quietly, "Away from you if you're gonna cry." I stood and wiped my tears. I followed Sukata closely until we reached the ladder to the roof. He looked at me and said, "Babies first," and began to chuckle. I glanced at him with a disgusted look and began to climb.

Once we reached the top, he asked, "Why the fuck were you over there to begin with?" I did not answer and continued to walk toward the table and chairs. When I made it to the chair,

I dropped into it. I then turned toward the table and said, "I didn't think you were coming back." He walked up to the chair, next to mine, grabbed it and scooted it approximately a meter away from mine and let go of it.

He set the machete, the shotgun, a pistol, a large survival knife, a jug of water, a box of ammunition, a bag of ammunition, and an M.R.E. on the table. He removed something from his back pocket and set it on the table in front of me. I stared at it for a moment and then picked it up. It was a map; the very map I was going to go to the general store to get.

I turned and looked at him. He just stared back at me. After a few moments, he asked, "Why didn't you come?" I looked at him confused. "I left you plenty of supplies and clues," he said. I stared at him confused for a moment and then replied, "What do you mean you left me plenty of supplies? You left a bottle of water, an M.R.E., my survival knife, and some medical supplies. What the hell did you expect me to do with that?" He just chuckled at my response.

He stood up, walked over to the one of the ventilation units, pulled up a panel to reveal an open cavity, reached in and pulled out my glaive, the box of M.R.E.s, the box of water bottles and jugs, a rifle, a large ammunition can, my bag, a bundle of blankets, and a tarp. He threw everything in one of the boxes and carried it over to the table. He set it all down and simply said, "You didn't look hard enough."

I stared at him, again with disgust. When he saw my facial expression, he just laughed and handed me an M.R.E. and a bottle of water. I looked at the pile of supplies and asked, "How the hell did you expect me to carry all of that?" He rummaged through the pile and pulled out my bag. He threw it at me and said, "I didn't. I expected you to carry what you could and leave the rest here as a cache. I knew you wouldn't be able to carry everything, that's why I only took what I needed and left the rest for you to choose from." I continued to stare at him with disgust and asked, "How the hell was I supposed to know where you were?" "I left you my map," is all he said.

I reached into my back pocket and retrieved the map that I found. I rolled it out and looked it over. After several moments of staring at it, searching for answers, I spotted it. In the small square, labeled 'General Store,' there was a star and an arrow pointing from the sewage facility toward the star. I looked at Sukata and asked, "How was I supposed to know that's what that meant? I couldn't tell heads from tails on this damn map." With a look of disappointment on his face he said, "You *are* like a child. Must I teach you everything? Must I treat you like a little brother?" He pointed at the map and explained, "The colors indicate the amount of infected that tend to roam that area; the darker the color, the more infected there are. The pencil marks indicate possible locations for supplies, the pen marks indicate possible locations for food, the marker indicates possible locations for potable water. And finally, the damn star and arrow mean that's where I went. How fucking hard was that to figure out?"

I sat there, taking everything in. After I had figured it all out,

I turned to Sukata who was setting his bag down. I said, "I thought, for sure, there was something more to it than that." He opened his bag and retrieved a lantern as he said, "The more simple something is, the less likely it is to fail. Stop over thinking everything and just do what needs to be done." He did not know, but those words would become my entire philosophy for survival.

He handed me the lantern and said, "Here, use this to write your tale. I have no need for it." He then set a can of lantern fuel on the table and said, "Ration it." Without another word, he stood and walked away. I sat there for several moments, then ate the M.R.E. and drank the water. When I finished, I said aloud, hoping Sukata would hear me, "I have so many questions to ask you about survival and everything." I heard no reply. I opened my notebook and put pen to paper, pouring my thoughts onto the blank page. It is quite late now; I must get some sleep. I have a feeling tomorrow will be a long day.

Log Entry 21

It has taken two days to get to the General Store. I was not able to write a log last night because we were constantly on the move. We did not rest until we, finally, reached our destination. I believe Sukata plans to stay here for a few nights, while scouting out the mall and pawnshop. I am unsure of his plans but I have confidence in him, for he has gotten us this far without any aid from me. He takes the term "one-man-army" literally.

I will attempt to recount all that happened during the last two days. Some parts may be more detailed than others, for some events were more vivid and traumatizing and as we traveled, I became weary and could not account for my surroundings as often.

Sukata awoke me long before first light. He had already gathered all of his chosen equipment and told me to select what I was taking. Glancing over the remaining equipment, I noticed my machete missing. I asked Sukata about it and he just stared at me. When I pointed at the machete, he simply said, "I fed you, I saved you, I helped you. I got your map and gave you something to look forward to. I have taken you under my wing when I could have left you for dead. I like this machete. And after doing all of that, all I ask is to use it, and you deny me this much?" I did not know how to reply. I stood there speechless for several moments before words finally came to my mouth. I said, "I didn't mean it like that. I was just wondering what the deal was. I know you've done a lot for me and the least I could do is give you my machete. But, I need something to fight with also." He stared back at the table and said, "I'll trade you, your machete, for that .22." After a few short moments of glancing back and forth, from the machete to the table, I asked, "And ammo?" His large hand rose and pointed at the ammunition box. He looked at me and replied, "There is plenty in there, carry what you may." I walked to the table picked up the rifle and turned back to Sukata. "I'll accept that deal," I stated. I turned back to the table and opened the box of ammunition. I scavenged through the box, finding all the .22 ammunition I could find.

He was not lying when he said there is plenty. Altogether, I found approximately eighty rounds and a spare magazine. Each magazine holds ten rounds. I loaded both and slipped one into the rifle and chambered a round. Sukata walked over to me, grabbed the rifle, ejected the magazine, loaded an additional round, and replaced it in the rifle. I looked at him with an expression that a student might give his teacher when taught something of significance.

He handed me the rifle and began walking toward the ladder. I asked him, "You're not waiting on me?" He simply looked at me and began climbing down the ladder. I hastened my pace and gathered all that I could carry that would be of use to me. I ran toward the ladder and looked down. Sukata was gone. I turned and began to climb down the ladder quickly. When I reached the bottom, I scanned my surroundings, looking for Sukata. When I turned to my left, he was less than a meter away, which startled me. He said, "Damn you're jumpy, now come on." With that, we were off.

The journey was a long one. We had traveled several

kilometers before we saw the highway. I had not realized it, but I had traveled further out of the suburbs in the first week I was out here than I thought. Sukata explained to me that we were actually about twenty kilometers from where I started. He said that the sewers make the trip seem shorter because they are a straight shot, but we cannot travel by sewer because there are too many, as he called them, "zombies." We had encountered several of the creatures, but only one at a time until midday. As we rounded a stone fence that followed alongside the highway, Sukata stopped. I walked a few more steps to see what he saw but he stopped me, placing his large hand in the center of my chest. I halted and waited, silently. After a few moments, I heard that unmistakable coughing noise. I lifted my glaive, readying myself. Sukata did not seem to move; he was as still as a statue. Then, suddenly, he swung the machete and blood splattered the wall-like fence. Startled, I stepped back and recollected myself. Closing my eyes, I tried to prepare myself for what may happen. When I opened my eyes, Sukata was standing in front of me, waving his hand in my face. He asked if I was alright and I replied with a yes.

He continued on. It took me a second to move but I quickly caught up. When I walked around the end of the fence, I saw eight or nine, severely mutilated bodies, nearly diced, strewn all over the highway, blood pooling around them. I stopped and stared in awe at the scene. Sukata turned and asked, "What's wrong?" I could not answer. He just shrugged his shoulders and kept walking.

After several kilometers, I asked him, "How did you do that?" He looked at me with a confused look, for it had been a few hours since we encountered the group. "How did you kill all of them so fast?" He stared at me and cracked a slight grin. "I wait for them to come to me. As they get close I swing and swing hard. They usually plow themselves through the blade, doing the work for me. Once I finish one off, I usually kick it away from me so that my boots don't get covered with infected blood. Why?" With a look of amazement, I asked, "Is that all? Really? Where did you learn that?" He looked at me and replied, "Yes. Really. And I taught myself. I learned a long time ago to let the enemy come to you, don't waste your energy going to them. Then when he does come to you, use him as a weapon against himself. Other peoples' mistakes can prove to be useful in a fight, if you know how to use them."

It was night before we encountered another group of the creatures. This time it was in a building while we were searching for a place to spend the night. It was a large building, approximately four stories tall. Sukata walked to the front entrance, peered through the window, and then knocked on the door. I watched him, noting his techniques. After a few moments, he set his ear to the door and listened. We stood there for, what seemed to be, eternity before he said "Sounds clear." Using a large rag, he wrapped his fist and forcefully punched the glass of the door. The glass shattered in a magnificent array of sparkles as the moonlight gleamed off it. He reached in and unlocked the door.

We entered, slowly and cautiously. Sukata explained that we

should not stop here unless we know for sure it is clear. He gave me instructions to stay at his back and pay attention to my surroundings. I listened and kept close, examining everything as we walked through the building.

We searched the lower floor, one room at a time, until we had covered every segment. Once we were sure the first floor was cleared, we moved toward the front of the building again. In the center of the building, in one of the corridors, we found a large staircase leading upward. Sukata walked up, step by step, looking upward at an angle, following the railing of the stairs. With his machete loosely hanging in his hand, he seemed as though he was going to drop it at any moment.

Suddenly, over the railing, a body fell toward us. Sukata sidestepped and swung, slicing the body into three parts as it fell; it was sundered at the waist and mid-face. It fell all the way to the basement level with a loud echoing crash of bones on concrete. My heart was beating so hard, I could only hear its thump in my ears. Sukata paused for a second and then looked down toward the body's resting place. He turned, looking at me with a concerned look on his face. I could read his lips, but could not hear him over the beating of my heart. His lips read, "Run! They're coming! And there's a lot of 'em!"

Without warning, Sukata bolted up the stairs, leaping over the steps three or four at a time. I could not move. I was frozen in place with shock. After a short moment, my heart slowed slightly and I could think more clearly. I heard the creatures' coughing, their feet pattering against the steps. Quickly, I ran after Sukata, climbing the stairs as fast as I could. I could not see Sukata nor could I hear him. At one point, I stopped and looked down the stairs, spotting a group of the creatures, and thought to myself, "There is no way I can out run these fucking things. I need to find a place to hide."

I ran up the stairs until I found an exit. I burst through the door, sweat spraying from my face. I slammed the door shut and turned the lock. In a hurry, I scanned the corridor for somewhere to hide. When I spotted a large vent at the end, to my right, I made a run for it. The corridor seemed so long, nearly endless.

Reaching the end, I used my glaive to rip the vent cover from the duct. I crawled inside, realizing it did not turn downward but instead, upward, toward the roof. I stood up, turned, and jumped, grabbing the corner of the bend in the duct. I pulled myself up, leaning forward, using my stomach to prop myself in the passage. I began to drag myself forward. My bag was causing it to be a tight squeeze.

I was nearly to the next bend, when I heard the door in the corridor smash open. My heart began to race as the adrenaline in my bloodstream increased. With newly found strength, I ripped myself to the turn in the duct, rolled onto my back and scooted, sitting up in the conduit.

Standing up, I could see another vent. I hopped over the corner and used my stomach, once again, to prop myself as I dragged myself toward the vent. Slow and tedious, the task became as I pulled with the palms of my hands, which were getting sweaty. The steel began to feel as though it were covered with oil as my hands began to slip.

After what seemed to be an eternity, I reached the vent. Pushing hard against the grate, I managed to break it loose from the wall and shoved it outward. I, hastily, crawled out and got to my feet. I was in another corridor; windows adorning both ends. Through the window to my left, I could the sun beginning to rise. I ran toward the source of the light as though it were my last hope.

As I neared the window, a door to my right burst open and a creature came running, while screeching, toward me. I quickly swung my glaive in a downward motion. The eyes of my victim were wide, hungry, emotionless, as though they foresaw such sacrifice. Slowly, the blade slid from the freshly manifested wound as my victim knelt before me; its hands clawing, grabbing; a last, hopeless, attempt to feed its hunger. My blade, long and sharp, fell to my side as though it were an extension of my own arm.

As blood trickled off my hand, it stained the steel upon which it fell as though the steel were ice. The body of my victim lay

motionless, still, with death. A sigh of passionate relief

slipped from my lips; too soon, I heard more coming; the

coughing sound, growing louder, as they neared. Their stench

burned an unforgettable smell into my nostrils.

Quickly, around the corner, turning right, I ran. I knew they

had already sensed me. I ran down the corridor, a left, a right,

another corridor, and finally a door. I burst out into the early

sunlight, onto a balcony; the fresh air, so sensual. This

pleasure could not be appreciated for long.

I heard them; ever so determined. Endless is their march.

Insatiable hunger drives them, nothing more. Demons, they

are, human in form but not in heart or soul; neither of which

they possess. Gathered in hordes they march, hunting,

searching for a creature to feed upon. As they walk, death lay

behind them; as though a disease, they would spread. A

plague hath not they brought, but they themselves are a

plague.

As locusts devour crop, they devour any living creature in

their path. As though they were insects, they obstruct every orifice of cities. A never ending cycle, for, as they feed, so do they multiply. Their bloodlust not to end until, all life has been undone. Sickening is the knowledge of their presence. Cold and twisted are their desires.

They are an army, the ultimate army, a tireless, senseless, mindless, fearless, unstoppable army. They walk, through infectious filth, through blistering heat, thirst less, they walk. Through frostbiting cold, sensationless, they walk. Upon broken limbs, over broken earth with the pads of their feet exposed, they walk. Upon their fleshless stomachs and severed torsos, they crawl. Continuously they march, for they know not of pain, of thirst, cold or heat, nor do they know of sympathy. Only of hunger do they know; an insatiable hunger.

I had to hurry, before they reached me, for if I allowed them to surround me…I do not want to even think about the fate that would have beheld me. I saw more on the ground below; their image so grotesque, their stench so overwhelming, their call nightmarish, their stare so lifeless, so heartless. A plague, this is what they are. A festering wound of infectious disease, rotting away into the very core of their empty, soulless shells. They are demons, demons stealing the very sanity of any man whom dare face them.

I ran to the edge of the balcony. To my left, I found a large pipe attached to the wall. I grabbed it with my right hand, climbed onto the ledge of the balcony and jumped to the pipe, hugging it tightly. I did not dare to look down and instead began to climb. I felt so weak when I finally reached the top. I grabbed the edge of the roof and without warning, something gripped my wrist. I panicked and almost let go.

I was being pulled up. When I could see over the ledge of the roof, Sukata was dragging me the remaining distance to the top. When I landed, I lay there for a moment, breathing hard. Sukata looked down at me and asked, "What happened to ya?" I could not speak, for I was still trying to catch my breath. He helped me to my feet and said, "Come on, we gotta go," and took off toward the rear of the building.

I slowly followed behind; as a marathon runner would cross the finish line. When we got to the rear, he pointed at a fire escape ladder and said, "Alright, here's the plan: we climb down, stop before we get to the ground, jump over to the shorter building; rest for a second and when I say second, I mean second; get over to that truck parked in the dock, climb onto the trailer, get to the front of the truck, climb down, and make a run for the highway." He pointed out each part of his plan as he explained and I nodded in acceptance.

We went through with his plan, nearly failing when we had to jump to the other building. Sukata barely made it; and had to catch me, otherwise, I would have become a feast for those creatures. Once we were on the roof of the smaller building, we ran toward the truck. We climbed the truck without any issues and got to the front and climbed down the side using the hood, fenders, and tires as steps.

Once we reached the ground, we ran as covertly as possible toward the highway. It was a hard run, for I was worn out and Sukata had to keep dragging me, wearing him down. It must have taken us nearly an hour to get to the highway but we managed. As we approached the edge of the highway, we saw a large box-truck with the rear door open. Cautiously, we investigated; finding a few boxes of energy drinks and snack cakes among the rubbish. Sukata offered me some and said that they would help keep my energy up. I accepted them and we ate and drink as we walked.

It was nearly sun down when the General Store came into view. We still had a few kilometers to go and we were exhausted. We had eaten and drank all of the snack cakes and energy drinks we had scavenged from the truck and our bodies were burning through more calories than we could replace. I felt as though I was I going to die if we did not stop soon.

It was well into night before we reached the General Store. Sukata used the same knocking technique as he explained that he had not seen many "zombies" in this area. When he felt it was safe, we entered. The store was nearly bare. There was no food or water. We searched the entire building. This time I was cautious about where I went; not straying far from Sukata. After all three rooms were cleared, we gathered what items we thought may be helpful and climbed, through the attic, onto the roof.

We sat here, resting for some time before we shared an M.R.E. and a bottle of water. I asked Sukata a few questions. He answered them and then lay down to sleep. I could not sleep, even though I was exhausted, and instead decided to write. It is nearly light again. I must get some rest before we travel again.

Log Entry 22

It has been a long day. Sukata and I used a pair of binoculars to scout as far as we could without getting off the roof. He told me that it is not good to stay in one place for very long, so he does not plan to stay here longer than he needs to. I was hoping that we would at least stay for a day or two, but I see now that that is not going to happen.

I believe, now for sure, that I am going mad. I found myself looking at my injured foot, hungrily, wanting to remove it. I did not feel like eating it, but instead simply removing it. I do not understand what brought about this train of thought. I also noticed that I had a strange feeling around Sukata. Not as though I am attracted to him, but instead something similar to that which a father figure would impose upon a young child. I know that I am not much younger than Sukata; however, he seems to be a big brother, of sorts, to me. Sukata keeps me in line and alive. He leaves me to discover my mistakes on my own but does not allow me to continue my self-assigned missions if they may endanger us. He also gives me advice, but only when I ask. He shows me things but never tells me how to do something, unless I ask. And he never lets me go too long without something to eat or drink if he can keep from it.

He keeps telling me, "The only reasons I keep you around are: A) It gives me someone to talk to. B) You may prove useful for certain things. C) I like the idea of having someone to help me if need be. D) I kind of like having someone around to watch my back when I sleep. And E) If all else fails, you'll make fine 'zombie bait.'" He always laughs at that last one as though he is joking, but I know he is not. It does not make me uncomfortable knowing that he would use me as bait, but it does worry me. I am afraid that he may actually use me as bait while I am still alive, but then again, he does not seem to be that kind of guy…that is, if he likes you.

I asked him why he was named Sukata. He only stared at me. When I asked him, "Who named you?" he said, "I did." I looked at him confused and asked, "You did? What's your

real name?" He stared at me and said, "That's not important."
I grinned thinking he was joking but he seemed to be serious.
After a few minutes, I asked, "Why don't you talk about your
past?" He looked up at the star-speckled sky and said, "The
past is what makes us who we are as of now. It does not
matter any further than that. If you like who you are, where
you are, how you are, what you are, or who you're with now,
the rest doesn't matter."

I did not ask him anymore questions about that subject and
instead asked about how he ended up in this situation. He
said, "I won't get into the details. I was sitting at home,
drawing a picture for a friend. I got up to go to the bathroom
and I heard something at the door. I was home alone so I
hurried to the door. When I opened the door, I usually put my
foot behind it just in case someone tries to force their way in.
The door slammed against my foot, breaking my toes. I
quickly shoved the door shut and locked it. I grab the nearest
knife I had laying around and checked through the window
next to the door to see who it was. There were three of them

outside my front door. I slowly unlocked the door, opened it just enough for one to come charging at me and stabbed it in the forehead. When I saw the other two tearing the dead one apart, I knew what I needed to do. I grabbed my bug-out bag, a few of my knives, and a couple machetes. I locked all of the windows and doors and headed to the bathroom. I filled every container I could find with water, then filled the tub and sinks. I bugged in for about a week before I realized I had to get somewhere. I got my shit and got out. I have been traveling since." He acted as though he did not want to talk about it any further, so I left the subject alone.

After a few minutes of awkward silence, I asked, "Well, can you tell me how you know all of the things you know? How about, where you're headed?" He sat there quietly for a few seconds, and replied, "I'm heading to New York. I learned everything I know through trial and error." I looked at him and asked, "What's in New York? And can you teach me?" He ignored the first question and said, "I have been teaching you." I stared at him confused for a moment and then realized he *had* been teaching me, I just did not know it.

We continued on like that, until well past dark. Sukata said that I should get some rest and clean my wounds, for I had not changed the bandages for a couple of days. I removed the bandages, noticing that my arm had healed over and that my foot had come a long way. I did not replace the bandage on my arm. I cleaned my foot well and wrapped it with a clean bandage and used some plastic from an M.R.E. package to wrap it again. Once I finished, I sat down, while Sukata continued to scout and began writing. It is nearly midnight, by position of the moon, so I am going to end it here, for tomorrow we travel.

Log Entry 23

I was awakened well before first light by a harsh screeching noise. I jumped up and ran to the edge of the roof, searching for the source. It took a few moments to realize what exactly I was looking at, but I soon figured it out. Hoping my eyes were fooling me, I shut them. When I opened them again, Sukata was standing over me, his right hand propped on his knee. He stared at me for a moment and then said, "You're even jumpy when you sleep."

I sat up and asked him how long he had been watching me. He simply looked me in the eye and said, "Long enough to kill you, not enough to know you." He laughed subtly as he stood up and offered his hand to help me to my feet. I grabbed his hand as though we were going to shake hands, my thumb wrapped around his, my fingers wrapped around the top of his thick wrist. He jerked me to my feet as though I were a child and light as a feather.

After I got my balance and cleared the crust from my eyes, I asked, "How long was I out?" Sukata pointed at the moon and said, "It has yet to move." I looked at him with confusion, "You mean a few minutes? How the hell do you function like that? I need more sleep." I lay back down but Sukata persisted, telling me about sleep deprivation and how to overcome it. I just listened, trying to stay awake, but eventually failed and passed out.

When I awoke, Sukata was gone and it was nearly midday. I looked around, trying to see if he left any clues. All of his equipment, except the machete, his cordage, and a jug of water, was still in the same location as the night before. I rolled to my back, let out a deep sigh, and got to my feet. I did not know where he went but, judging by what he took with him, he was not far.

I grabbed the binoculars and began scanning the areas of the mall and pawnshop. I did not see any signs of him nor did I see any signs that he may have been through there. I kept an eye out, watching for anything out of the ordinary. It seemed as though he had not left but instead, was in the building beneath my feet.

After a while of searching, I happened to notice an eerie calm about this part of the city. I had not heard such peace since before the outbreak. I did not feel comfortable with the silence and began to fidget with the binoculars. I could barely contain myself. I set the binoculars down and climbed into the attic of the General Store. I walked to the ladder, leading to the lower floor, and climbed down. When I set foot on the floor, I heard something behind me.

Snatching my knife from its sheath with lightning speed, I turned. It was nothing; there was nothing; I had just been hearing things. I calmed myself down and began to walk through the corridor toward the front of the store. As I neared the door separating the rear room, which I was in, and the main area of the store, I heard it again. I turned around, searching, listening. I found nothing. I stood there listening and watching for movement. I did not see or hear anything and turned around to continue on.

As I turned, something caught my attention from the corner of my eye. I jerked my head in the direction of the movement. I did not see anything, but kept watching. I listened carefully. I could hear a small child laughing. I began to walk toward the source of the noise. I was cautious, watching my surroundings as I walked.

As I turned to enter the other room of the building, I could hear the laughter get louder. I stepped into the room, slowly. I scanned for anything that may peak my interest. I did not see anything. I took another step in. I scanned again, listening carefully. I did not hear or see anything. I waited a moment. Hearing the laughter again, I turned toward the small closet that occupied the opposite side of the room. I took a step toward it.

"What are you doing?" Sukata asked, scaring the shit out of me. I turned around quickly, finding him in the doorway. I said, "I heard a child laughing. I was just seeing what it was." He looked at me as though I had something wrong with my face and said, "Alright, then why are you heading toward a closet with blood pouring out of the bottom?" I turned to look at the closet. He was right; there was a massive pool of blood gathered at the base of the door. How could I have missed it? I stared at it in confusion for a few moments and then turned back to Sukata. He was already gone.

I walked to the door and searched the corridor; he was nowhere to be found. I turned back to the closet, asking myself, "Are you going mad?" I walked toward the closet and stretched my arm out to turn the door knob. My fingers slid along the cold metal as they wrapped around it. I began to slowly turn the knob. The door clicked, signaling the bolt had shifted far enough for the door to open. I slowly, carefully, opened the door. The hinges creaked as the gap became larger. I could hear the laughing getting louder, the further the door opened. The gap had grown to nearly two-hundred-fifty centimeters when, suddenly, a bunch of bloody fingers grabbed the edge of the door.

I could hear Sukata telling me to wake up. I opened my eyes, finding him standing over me. I asked, "What...what happened?" He looked at me and replied, "I was hoping you could tell me that. I came back after going off to see if I could find a better path to the mall than the road and, when I came back, you were gone. I searched around for you and finally found you laying here, out cold." I looked at him and then looked around. I looked back at him and said, "I just had the weirdest dream…" He looked at me with a blank face and asked, "What the hell were you doing in the closet?" I looked down toward my feet, between which I could see the closet door open. I stared at it for a moment and noticed there was no blood on the floor and the door was completely open.

I turned back to Sukata and said, "That door wasn't open like that and there was blood all over the floor." He stood up and simply said, "You need sleep or help. I don't know which one, but I do know which one I can help you with." He pounded his right fist into his left hand jokingly. I told him that I was alright and that I could manage.

I stood up and began to walk back toward the roof. When I reached the ladder to climb into the attic, I spotted small streaks of blood ornamenting the rungs. I turned to look at Sukata and asked, "Where did these come from?" He walked to the ladder and examined the marks. "I don't know," he said as though it were nothing of significance. Confused, I followed Sukata up the ladder into the attic. When I reached the top, I saw it.

It seemed as though an angel had descended upon us. It seemed to be the most beautiful thing I had ever seen. There lying on the attic floor, in a small pool of blood, was a young deer. There were no gunshot wounds nor were there any broken limbs. I looked at Sukata and then it, again. Sukata said, "I got this little bastard th'smorning. I saw him running down the street and climbed down from the roof. I waited at the front door until he came running by and stabbed him." Amazed by Sukata's feat, I asked, "How?" He just said, "A lil' bit o' luck and a lil' bit o' skill. I was amazed I managed it myself." At that moment, I could feel the world melting away, taking all of our problems and worries with it. I knew it would not last but for that one moment, for that singular moment in time, I felt as though everything was going to be alright.

We skinned the deer out and cut the meat into thin strips. We ate our fill and lay the rest out on the roof to dry. Sukata said that it may spoil before it dries and that we will have to keep an eye on it. He said that if we had salt or a smoker, it would not be too big an issue. He also told me that the meat would not hold longer than a week, maybe two, but that that is much longer than if we had not dried it.

I enjoyed the meal, wishing that we could eat that way every day. I wished that we had more water, for then we would have been able to better enjoy our meal. It was hard to choke down the raw meat without something to follow it with. Despite that, the meal was the best I had had in almost three weeks.

Once all was taken care of, Sukata and I sat down and hashed out a plan to get to the pawnshop and mall. After much debate, we decided to go to the pawnshop first, for there may be much needed weapons and ammo. After we finished with the pawnshop, we would make our way to the mall. Sukata said that it may be suicidal trying to get into the mall, even if it would be worth the risk. He explained that if the danger becomes too great or gaining access would prove to be too difficult or too risky, we would abandon the mission and continue on our way.

We took inventory of our equipment. Here is a list of our possessions: One .22 rifle, approximately seventy-six .22 rounds, a spare .22 magazine, approximately a week worth of water, eight M.R.E.'s, one 12-gauge shotgun, thirty 12-gauge shotgun shells, a machete, a makeshift glaive, two backpacks, two rolls of gauze, approximately two-hundred milliliters of iodine, four large gauze pads, a small sewing kit, approximately ten meters of random cordage, approximately fourteen meters of parachute cord, a small lantern, a small can of lantern fuel, a tarp, a roll of newspaper, a state map, a hand-drawn map of the city, a nine millimeter pistol, twenty-eight nine millimeter rounds, a partial roll of duct tape, and an unknown amount of soon-to-be deer jerky.

After we finished taking inventory, we gathered all of our things, sorting them as we packed our bags. We prepared everything to leave tomorrow night, for by then the meat should be nearly dried, if it does not rain. We checked everything over and set our bags near the center of the roof. When all was finished, Sukata and I sat down and told jokes trying to lighten our mood and take our minds off of the hell which we would have to endure the next night.

Log Entry 24

We are stranded inside a large building. We may not be able to get out short of a small miracle. The means by which we landed ourselves in such a situation are simple, yet seemingly complex. Had we taken note of a minute detail, we would not be in the position we are...

Sukata and I awoke approximately the same time. He had been sitting, watching the pawnshop for a few moments before I awoke. When he heard me stir, he explained to me that he had not seen any movement near the pawnshop, however, there was something inside the building itself. He could not make it out, but it seemed to be watching back. He said that it looked almost human, but it had not moved since he spotted it.

He kept watching the unknown subject until I had gotten everything else together. Once I had everything setup and ready to go, he stood and began checking the meat. I looked at him and asked, "Is it going to work?" He looked up at the sky off in the distance, took a deep breath and said, "If it doesn't rain this afternoon, we should be able to dry it the rest of the way before we leave." I looked in the direction he had, seeing nothing of significance, I asked, "What d'you mean? The skies are clear." He shook his head and grinned slightly, "Much to learn, much…to…learn."

He turned back toward the pawnshop and returned the binoculars to his face. After a few short moments, he got a little excited and began to shift positions to change the angle of view. Watching him, I noticed his reactions were becoming those of concern. I kept silent for some time until he lowered the binoculars. He turned to me as I began to ask, "What is it?" He simply walked to the neatly assorted equipment and grabbed the .22 rifle. Walking back to his former position, he checked the chamber, ensuring a round was loaded.

I started toward him as he raised the rifle to his shoulder. There was no scope on the rifle, so he could not be using it for such a purpose but, instead, must have spotted something which would be worth using ammunition. He stood there, still for a moment, and then slowly squeezed the trigger. The rifle reported with a sharp popping noise, ringing out across the open range in which he fired. He did not move, remaining in his initial stance, and fired once more.

I looked toward the pawnshop, in hope of seeing what it was he was shooting. I could not see what he had seen. I waited for an explanation but none came. Sukata set the rifle down on the roof next to his feet and raised the binoculars to his face again. He remained silent, for what seemed hours, as I waited in suspense.

I could not bear it anymore and asked him what he was doing. He lowered the binoculars and turned to me with a grin, to one side, on his face. I stared at him for a moment before he responded, "I got it." I continued to stare, waiting for more details. He did not supply any and, instead, bent down to grab the rifle and began walking toward the equipment. Disappointed, I asked, "What? What did you get?" Sukata stopped and said, "Whatever was looking back."

Shocked, I became speechless. I could not think clearly. I stood there watching Sukata as he reloaded the rifle's magazine and then replaced the rifle. It took several moments to come to my senses. When I could finally think clearly, I asked with excitement, "What if it 'was' a human? What if it was an actual person…not one of those creatures or a mannequin? Wha…" He cut me off replying, "Oh well." I stared at him as though he were not human; something not of this world; an alien. I began to walk toward him as he stood and turned toward me. I got nearly nose to nose with him and shouted, "What do you mean 'Oh well.'?! How can you even say such a thing?! That could've been someone's parent or child!"

Without hesitation, he replied, "It 'was' someone's child and if it 'was' a parent, it's too late now!"

I could not help myself and began to shout again, "It wouldn't be too late if you didn't shoot it to begin with! I can't fucking believe you! I…" I turned and walked away, toward the attic window, before I got too carried away.

Sukata walked the opposite direction, toward the pawnshop; I could hear his footsteps slowly fade. I sat down, my feet hanging off the edge of the roof, and began to think about what he had just done. I could not believe someone could be so cold. I felt as though my heart had broken.

After gathering my thoughts, I returned to Sukata with an argument he could not defy. I started in well before I reached him, "How can someone be so cold?! How can you shoot something and not care?! Why?!..."

I do not remember the rest. I awoke in the late afternoon, my face hurting, and barely able to breathe through my nose. I sat up and looked around. Sukata had not moved from his post and there was a small pool of blood on the roof near him. I was only a meter or so away from him and the blood was nearly to my left boot. I asked, "What the hell?" He turned and looked at me, "Get enough sleep?" He stood and walked over, offering his hand again. I accepted and let him lift me to my feet. I touched my face, letting out a moan of pain. He told me to hold still and tilted my head back, examining my face. After a moment, he said, "Yup, I think I broke it," and let go of my head. I looked at him with astonishment. He did not say anything further and walked over to the meat scattered on the roof.

I stood there, watching him. I did not know whether to be angry or just shut up before he hit me again. After thinking it over, I asked, "Why?" Without looking at me, he asked, "Why what?" I expanded, "Why did you hit me?" "Because, you wouldn't shut up," he replied. "So you fucking knock me out?" I questioned. "That's how I handle things. Is there a problem with that?" he asked as he turned to look at me. I quickly replied, "No...no...no problem, I just wished you would use a different method...like asking." He did not respond and turned back to the meat.

"It's not going to be dry. It's about to rain and it still has a few hours to go. Grab what you can and stuff it in the bags, we're taking off in a few minutes," Sukata explained. I had not noticed but the sky was quite cloudy and I could see a light sprinkle beginning. I did not believe it; Sukata was right about the rain. I walked over to aid him in collecting the meat.

Once all of it had been gathered, we crammed as much as possible into every crevice of the bags. Approximately three-fourths of it still remained, so we stuffed our pockets, and used some cordage to wrap the rest into bundles. We tied the bundles to our bags, grabbed the rest of our gear and began to climb down.

As we neared the front door of the store, the rain came hard. Sukata turned to me and without a word we walked to the counter and laid out our plan in the dust. We would exit the store, run down the street, using the sound of the rain to cover the sound of our footsteps and any cars and other objects to hide. When we reached the pawnshop, we would not be able to use the knock technique, so we would simply break in by knocking out a window and unlocking the door. We both agreed on the plan and knew to be ready for anything when we entered the pawnshop; for we had no time to investigate it before we entered.

We bolted out the front door, hitting one of the creatures with the door as it swung open. Sukata quickly stabbed it in the forehead before it could react and began running again. We were approximately four blocks from the pawnshop, three of which were an overflow parking lot for the train station; the last block being a large duck pond. We ran as quickly as we could, ducking behind vehicles, mailboxes and such whenever possible.

It seemed as though we would be able to get to the pawnshop without any trouble. I began to feel confident that we were going to make it without having to fight but, when we stopped near the pond, I spotted a large group of the creatures coming from the train station. I patted Sukata on the shoulder and pointed at the group. Without looking, he said, "I know, I'm trying to figure this out." I began to feel nervous. Sukata remained crouched and began jogging toward the pond. I quickly followed.

At the edge of the pond, he stopped and pulled one of the bundles of meat from his bag. He looked at me and said,

"They smell us." He threw the meat toward the parking lot and grabbed the other bundle from his bag and threw it across the street. He had me turn around and removed both bundles from my bag and hurled them toward the crowd. The creatures became frantic as they all attempted to devour the bundles at once. Sukata said, "That oughta hold 'em," and started for the pawnshop again.

As we neared the entrance of the store, Sukata grabbed his machete, high on the handle, with his right hand. With fluid motion, he walked to the door, broke the glass with the hilt of the machete, and reached in; unlocking the door with his left hand. As he shoved the door open, I turned to see where the group was. Walking into the building, still looking behind me, I could see the creatures as they found the first bundles thrown. I hurried to close the door and lock it again.

I turned around, finding Sukata unlocking an inner door that hindered us from entering the lobby of the store. Within a few short moments, Sukata had the door open and we entered. It was dark and we could not see very well.

I removed the lantern from my bag and lit it, using the built-in ignition.

As the light cast across the room, we could see massive amounts of dried blood decorating nearly everything. There were no guns; no weapons of any kind. There were several electronics and other items that were of no use to us; all of which seemed to be nearly destroyed. It looked as though someone had tried to salvage parts from many of the electronics, while others seemed to be built from the salvaged parts.

Sukata walked further into the store. I turned to my right, casting light upon a body with a bullet wound in its chest. The body was fresh. I stared at it for a moment then realized it was the thing Sukata was shooting at earlier. I knelt down, examining it further.

I discovered another bullet wound in the top of its head. I turned to Sukata, sorrow filling my heart, and said, "See? It 'was' a human, you fuck." He turned to me and looked at the body. Without expression or emotion, he said, "Oh well." I became quite angry and stood.

Sukata walked over to the body and searched it for anything useful. He found a cigarette lighter, a small .308 pistol with three rounds of ammunition and a small Swiss-Army knife. He stood up and said, "It's a she if you're wondering." Still angry, I looked at him and asked, "What, now you're molesting the body too?" He just looked at me and said, "Any moron can tell those are boobs, you fucking puss. Shut the fuck up about me killing her. What would you have done if she shot one of us trying to get in here, huh? It's for the better that we didn't have to deal with her, besides that would just be another mouth to feed and we're already running it tight." Seeing his point, I calmed down a bit, but that did not excuse the fact that he killed her and did not care.

After our short argument, Sukata said, "We need to search this place and find something to fix your nose." I nodded with agreement and began roaming the shop. As I came to a door near the back, I called for Sukata. I waited for a few moments, but he did not reply, so I continued on. I walked to the door and tested the knob. It was unlocked, but it seemed a little stiff. I did not force the door but instead tried to slowly shove it open. I heard something click and squeal on the other side of the door. Quickly I stopped and stepped back. Listening, I heard, what sounded like, a small engine start and a light began to flicker in the room on the other side. A tense moment passed and the light stopped flickering. I waited to the count of three before I started toward the door again. As I touched the door, the lights in the store began to flicker. Sukata yelled, "What the fuck?!" And I began to panic. I backed away from the door and turned around. Sukata was standing there, staring at me. He asked, "What the fuck did you do?!" I explained, "I just pushed this door open and shit started happening!" I could hear a loud clanking noise; Sukata must have also, for he turned to investigate the noise. After a few seconds the noise quit and was replaced by metal sliding, similar to that of a guillotine. I watched in shock as large sheets of metal came crashing down to the floor from the ceiling.

Sukata turned back to me and began walking toward me. I braced myself, expecting to be hit again. He shoved me to one side and kicked the door, I pushed, open. He walked in, looked around, and said, "Goddamn it! Emergency generator. She had this setup like a panic room...She would run to this room, which, when opened, would trigger the damn generator, and the security system would kick on and shut the place up like a box! I can't believe this shit!" He came charging out of the room at me. He stopped just in front of me and pointed his finger in my face with an angry look on his.

I stood there quiet. I knew that he knew I did not make a mistake, for how was I supposed to know the door was rigged, but he was still angry at me because I was at fault for triggering it. He did not say anything, just stood there angrily pointing at me and then turned and squatted, grabbing his head. I knew he was at a loss.

I squatted down next to him. He did not move at first, but eventually put his hands down and turned his head to face me. He said as calmly as he could, "Now we need to figure out how the fuck to get out of here." I looked him in the eye and said, "I will find a way if it's the last thing I do, I promise. This was my fuck up, I know." With that he seemed to calm quite a bit. He stood and replied, "You didn't make a mistake but I appreciate you accepting responsibility for your actions."

We entered the, as Sukata called it, panic room and searched everything. We found several rifles and pistols, but very little ammunition for any of them. We also found about a week's worth of water and a couple days' worth of food. In a small tool box, we discovered a surgical kit and a single shot "zip gun" (that is what Sukata called it) that had a 12-gauge slug in it. I wondered why such a thing would be in a medical kit and Sukata explained, "Sometimes that's the only medicine to fix your problems."

Disturbed by his comment, I walked to the body in the front of the store. She looked happy, like she had died with a grin on her face. I stared at her for a few moments then sat down next to her. Thinking about what Sukata had said, I began to think that he may have done her a favor by killing her. I did not like the idea of being in such a situation, but I could not say that I would not have wished for the same, for I did not know what she had endured.

Sukata called for me, so I stood and walked to the 'panic room.' Entering, I saw Sukata knelt down before the generator, holding a large box. I looked at him confused. "Where did you find that?" I enquired. He did not look at me, but pointed to a large hole in the floor with a pile of boards that had once been part of the floor lying next to it. I watched as he opened the box. Inside, there were several pictures, an enormous ammo box, and a rifle case. Sukata said, "By the weight, I know what this is," with a smile on his face.

He handed me the pictures and pulled the rifle case out. I flipped through the pictures, recognizing the dead woman in many of them. The others I was unsure of, but assumed they were her family. I forgot about the rest of the items Sukata had found as I fell deep into thought while studying the pictures. I turned and walked back to the body. I sat down next to her and continued to flip through the photos.

When I found one with the woman and some children standing in front of a house, I flipped the photo over as though I was showing her and asked, "Is this your family? I bet they were nice. I bet you were nice." I turned the photo back toward me to look at it again. While studying the photo, imagining myself meeting the family, I felt something touch my right knee. I moved the photo to see what it was, but found nothing. Assuming it was a phantom sensation, I flipped to the next photo.

This one had the family playing at the pool; but she was not in the picture. I turned the photo to her and asked, "You were taking the picture weren't you?" I turned it back toward me, looked at it for a moment, and then turned it back to her. "Are those your kids?" I questioned. She of course, did not reply, so I flipped to the next photo. As I stared at the photo, I noticed something that looked like a man pointing a gun toward the family, in the background. Staring at the photo, concentrating, I felt something brush my knee again. I moved the photo to see what it was; nothing. I ignored it and turned the photo to the woman. I asked, "Did something bad happen that day?"

The woman replied, "Yesh." I jumped, panicking. I stared at the body lying on the floor, her eyes were still open and she still had that strange grin on her face. I touched her with my foot; nothing. I stepped back and closed my eyes. When I opened them, the woman's head was turned slightly staring straight at me. I panicked and closed my eyes again. When I opened them the second time, the body was in the same position that I had found her the first time; she had not moved and her head was still facing slightly to her left, while I stood at her right.

Freaked out, I walked back to the 'panic room.' Sukata was holding a massive rifle, loading the magazine with rounds that looked like miniature missiles. He looked up at me with a smile on his face and said, "Fifty cal. Always wanted one." I stood in the doorway admiring the massive piece of equipment. Sukata slid the bolt up and back, chambering a round with a powerful clunk and raised the rifle to his shoulder, looking through the scope.

I removed my bag and walked to the corner, opposite the door, and sat down. I pulled my notebook from my bag and began writing. I do not know if I am actually going mad or if I am simply imagining things due to the stress of living the way we have to. I may not be able to figure it out on my own and can only hope that it passes.

Log Entry 25

It was a long night. Neither Sukata nor I slept. We tried several times to find a switch or other form of mechanism to reverse the lock down that the security system had employed, to no avail. Sitting in the 'panic room,' Sukata and I did come up with a plan; however, it would kill us or worse: attract an excessive amount of attention to our location. Trying to avoid the consequences of the first plan, we attempted to hash out another.

After several attempts and many failures, we came to the conclusion that we only had three options: A) Just stay here until we run out of food and water, then attempt to escape or wait it out until we die. B) Try our first plan, which involved using the .50 rifle he had found to blow holes in the steel and then attempt to knock a hole big enough for us to get out, given we are not dead from the percussion of the rifle in such a small building or the bullets hitting the steel. Or C) Find another way out of the building without relying on getting the lock down lifted.

I found the last to be our best option but Sukata and I have tried and failed every time. I do believe however, that there must be an emergency exit that is not affected by the lock down. I have yet to figure out where such an exit would be, but I am not giving up hope just yet.

Log Entry 26

We managed to make it to the mall. However, we are in another small building, I believe used for storage purposes, outside the mall. I have no idea what Sukata has planned but I believe we are going to try to get into the mall via the ventilation system near the rear. I feel Sukata has figured out a way to do it safely. I will talk to him about it later. For now, I need to record our experience up to this point.

We sat in the 'panic room' waiting for a decent plan to come to mind. When nothing better had been conceived, I began to roam around the store. I moved slowly from area to area, searching for any sign of a trap door or other hidden exit. It took several hours before I finally reached the woman's body.

I stared at it, ensuring myself she had not moved. I took note of her features, trying to convince myself she was human, not one of those creatures. She had long, deep brown hair, green eyes, as bright as an emerald with a light cast through it, skin that was fair, yet darkened by filth. She was of was fair height, I would estimate to be approximately one meter and seven-hundred-fifty centimeters. Her face was slender and her body figure seemed subtly curved, yet starved.

Her clothes were ragged and torn, exposing some of her midsection, revealing a belly piercing. Her feet looked as though she had walked across broken glass or sharp rocks. Her hands had a sense of rough use upon them. Altogether, I got the feeling she had been through hell and back, I knew that she had endured.

I turned away from her, searching the shelf above the counter. I was moving some of the objects around, trying to find anything of significance. At one point, I had to stand on my toes to reach something on the highest shelf. As I grabbed the item, which resembled a bomb, the lights began to flicker. I stopped and looked around.

As I turned my head to the left, I felt something against the bottom of my boot. I looked down toward the floor, finding the woman grabbing at my heel. I panicked and dropped the item on the counter. Almost instantly, the lights went out. I almost let out a shrill scream, but caught myself before it was forced out.

Sukata came into the room; I could hear his footsteps as he walked across the wooden floor. I stood quietly for a moment then lowered my feet to the floor. Sukata did not speak, he simply stood quietly. I turned slightly to face him, even though I could not see him. I explained that I had not done anything, but I did find a bomb-looking item.

Without a word, he walked further toward the entrance of the pawnshop. I could not see him, but could hear the creaking of the metal plate. I stood patiently waiting to see what was going to happen. The moment was tense and the suspense was killing me. I did not know whether that woman was alive and going to grab me again or if, when the metal sheet was lifted, those creatures were going to be awaiting us.

Sukata let out a hoarse grunt as he forced the steel plate upward, opening it, a centimeter at a time. I watched, in astonishment, as light began to pour through the crack; amazed at the sheer power Sukata possessed. It felt as though

I was watching a gorilla rip open a garage door. I could not say anything; I was at a loss for words.

Once the plate was raised enough for Sukata to slide under, he dropped to the floor and scanned outside. He turned his head to me and said, "Let's get moving.'" I did not hesitate as I followed his every move. He slid under the door with ease, me sliding right next to him as though we were attached at the hip.

Once we were on the other side, Sukata did not stop and quickly unlocked the external door. I followed close behind, plowing through the door into the blinding sunlight. I halted for a moment; I could not see where I was going or what was near me. I could hear Sukata running still, his feet hitting the pavement, hard, as he ran.

As my vision cleared, I noticed why Sukata was running. The large group of the creatures that we had encountered on our way to the pawnshop was slowly getting closer, walking through the duck pond. I could not believe my eyes and hesitated.

Finally, I got my wits about me and took off after Sukata. I did not look back for fear of seeing the creatures gaining on us. It took a few moments, but I eventually caught up with Sukata. We ran until the mall came into view and spotted a horde of the creatures.

As soon as Sukata noticed them, well before I did, he turned and ran toward the rear of the mall. It felt like an eternity as we ran, not knowing if any of the creatures had seen us. We continued to run until we reached this small building we are in now. Sukata hatched a plan while he ran.   Sukata, reaching the door of the building, jumped into the air and planted both feet on the door, completely removing it from its hinges. As the door fell, it seemed as though Sukata continued to run, never stopping, continuing on into the building. I fell behind as I attempted to raise the door back to its frame.

Without a word Sukata had ran back and grabbed me, saying, "Fuck that, we gotta go." We ran to the rear of the building, into an office-like room, and slid a filing cabinet we found against the door. Sukata stopped, breathing hard, and said between breaths, "We gotta…get…to the…roof…and…scout…the…place…out." I nodded in agreement, breathing as hard as Sukata. We sat down and thought our plan through.

Once we settled on a route, we left the room and began searching for stairs or a ladder. After several moments of searching, I spotted a ladder against the back wall and called for Sukata. We ran toward the ladder, relieved to see such. Breathing hard, we reached the ladder and began to climb. As I reached the third rung, I heard the door come crashing to the ground as those creatures began to pour into the building. Sukata climbed faster as I hurried him up the ladder.

Reaching the top of the ladder, a hatch hindered us. Sukata did not hesitate and shot the lock off with the small .308 pistol he had found. He burst out through the hatch, turned, grabbed my hand, and jerked me up onto the roof. He slammed the hatch shut and dropped his bag on top of it. He ran to the edge of the roof with the .50 rifle he had found and began to scope the area.

I sat down and caught my breath, drank some water, and lay down. Sukata came over, got a drink of water, and sat down. I sat up and turned to look at him. He simply grinned and said, "We did her." I replied, "Yes, yes we did." He laid his rifle down and grabbed an M.R.E. from his bag. He threw the M.R.E. at me and told me to get it ready. I did so as he searched the roof.

When we finished eating, I asked Sukata why he did not get the door open sooner. He explained that while the power was on, he would not have been able to; for the motors that held it in place were still running. But once they stopped, all he had to do was put enough pressure on them to turn them back. I told him thank you for everything he had done for me and retrieved my book and began writing.

Log Entry 27

We scouted the area until it was near dusk. When Sukata felt that most of the creatures were in the building, he told me gather my things and prepare for a run, going over his plan. I insisted that we find another way, but he refused to cooperate and told me that he would explain later.

I gathered my things, reluctantly, and Sukata grabbed his bag and rifle. We went to the side of the building where there was a guttering system that led, nearly, to the ground. We climbed over the edge of the roof and used our feet to hold ourselves to the guttering. Slowly, we lowered ourselves down, grabbing the guttering with our hands and began to slide down.

Approximately four meters from the ground, the guttering made a sudden turn. Sukata was the first to reach the bend and tested it. He looked up at me and said, "I don't think it's gonna hold." I looked down, trying not to look at the ground and replied, "What are we gonna do then?" He simply shrugged his shoulders and said with a careless and spontaneous tone, "Fuck it!" And with that, he began walking across it as though it were a ledge.

I lowered myself to the bend and stopped, watching Sukata. He seemed as though he was recklessly fearless and continued across the guttering as though he knew it would hold. I was cautious, only applying small amounts of my weight at a time, testing it. When I felt it may hold my weight, I stepped onto it. Centimeter by centimeter, I made my way toward Sukata.

Nearly to the corner of the building, Sukata turned to me and said, "It's holding thus far." I did not respond and continued watching my steps. I began to feel nervous when I heard a creaking noise beneath me. I told Sukata that I believed he spoke to soon and that we needed to hurry. He seemed to ignore me and continued on, rounding the corner of the building.

As Sukata disappeared around the building, I felt the guttering begin to give. I felt sick, knowing that I could fall to the ground at any moment. I hurried myself, trying to get to the end. I heard Sukata saying something to me but I could not make out what it was. I began to move faster, walking as fast as I could. As I made it to the corner of the building, I could hear Sukata clearly, "Stop! Stop you fuck, you're causin' it to give!"

I stopped immediately, but it was too late. The guttering slowly angled downward, creaking as it sloped faster and faster. I tried to keep my footing, but failed, sliding along the slope. Grabbing at the metal guttering as I slid, trying to hold on, I felt my finger catch something. Intense pain began to shoot up my arm as I began to slide faster. I looked upward, trying to avoid looking at the ground.

Blood was everywhere. It seemed as though someone had dumped a bucket of blood all over the side of the building in a long streak following the guttering. I could not help but let out a scream as I felt my feet fall free. Feeling my legs slip off, a sense of dread rushed through me. At that moment, I lost all hope in surviving.

Falling is a strange sensation. It feels similar to what one would imagine flying would feel like. The sensation of being gravity free, as though floating and yet being drawn to something, sends a tingling rush of adrenaline coursing through one's blood. It seemed as though eternity would pass and I would continue to fall, as though time itself had ended. My life began to flash before my eyes. I could see my family, my friends, and even my acquaintances. I felt as though, for that short moment, I could make amends with those I had hurt and hold those that I loved, if but only one last time. I then felt the dread of death, ever so, creeping in at the edges of my vision. I knew I was going to die, but I did not know when, for I had been falling for some time.

Finally, I landed, hard. I felt the air leave my body forcefully and could not breathe. My ribcage felt as though someone had stomped it flat as though it were a soda can and my head seemed as though it were split into two. I could not move nor could I feel anything. I was numb, completely numb. I began to become fearful, thinking I was paralyzed. My ears were ringing; I could not hear anything around me. My vision became blurred and I could not focus.

Someone appeared in the corner of my eye. They did not say anything, for their lips did not move, as they walked to me. They squatted down, grabbed my back pack and began dragging me. I could see some of the creatures coming around the edge of the building, only making out their silhouettes. My vision slowly became darker, until finally, complete blackness.

I awoke in a large room. It was so dark; I could see nothing. I looked around me, searching for anything I could see; nothing. I could not even see my own chest when I tilted my head down. I sat there quietly, hoping it was only a dream. I then, began to wonder, 'Is this what "they" see? Am I blind? Am I one of those creatures?' Many thoughts entered and left my mind. I could not focus.

I could feel an intense pain in my right leg, near the foot, and in my left hand. I could feel my hands behind my back, tied with something thin. I attempted, several times, to feel what it was that bound me. Eventually, I determined that it must be some form of wire. It began to lacerate my wrists, blood pouring down my hands.

As I sat there, my ability to think faded. I slowly slipped into a sleep; I assume from the loss of blood. I was going to die. Death did not hurt. It felt calming. It felt as though I was having the most sensual relaxation I had ever felt. It felt wonderful. It felt peaceful. I am at a loss for words to describe such a feeling. I feel I have failed.

A bright light appeared, blinding me. After a few moments, my eyes focused. I could see the silhouette of someone standing in a doorway. It walked toward me. I could not speak, for my throat was so dry, I felt as though I had drank sand. I attempted to raise my head; failed. I was too weak to look at whomever it was standing before me.

The figure knelt down, its left hand folded upon its leg as though it were using it as an arm rest. With its right hand, it reached down, grabbing my right ankle. I let out a grunt of pain as the bone crunched and grinded. I knew then, my ankle was broken.

The figure let go, walked to my left side, and knelt again. It reached behind me; I could feel its hand upon mine. It stood and walked out without a word; closing the door as it walked out, hurling me into a blackened world once more.

It felt as though an eternity had passed before the door was opened again; the bright light flooding the room, blinding me again. I attempted to raise my head, once more, failing. A figure appeared in the light and began walking toward me. I sat quietly, dreading what may become of me.

The figure, once more, knelt before me. I stared, nearly unconscious as it reached down, grabbing my ankle again. I let out a grunt of pain once again. The figure did not stand this time, instead, it twisted my ankle slowly. Intense pain shooting up my leg, I gave a shrill cry of agony. The figure let go of my leg and another figure entered the room.

The second figure was female, judging by her form. She walked to my left side and knelt down, setting something metal on the floor. I sat, fearful, waiting. She reached behind me, cutting my bindings free. I was too weak to move, my arms falling to my sides. The first figure spoke, revealing itself to be a male. I could not understand what he was saying, for my hearing was…"fuzzy."

The woman bandaged my left wrist and I felt her removing a bandage from my hand. After she replaced the bandage on my hand, she stood and walked to my right side. As she knelt, I heard the metal clank against the floor again. She grabbed my right arm and bandaged my wrist. When she finished, she turned to my ankle.

As she grabbed my pant leg, slowly pulling it up to expose my ankle, the man put his hand in front of her, signaling her to stop. He then pointed to the door, signaling her to leave. He never turned his eyes from me.

Once the woman exited the room, he asked in a menacing tone, "Where is your friend?" I could not reply, screaming, "I don't know!" in my head. He grabbed my ankle again, squeezing it. I grunted loudly, from my throat, in pain. He said to me, "We know about your friend, so just tell us and we can make all your pain end," patting the holstered pistol on his side. I remained quiet, fearful of what may happen to me.

When I did not reply, he asked, "Hmmm…thirsty aren't you?" I could not nod my head to answer him. He reached behind him, retrieving a canteen from his back. I looked at the canteen as though it were made entirely of gold. He seemed to be grinning as he opened it and took a drink, saying, "Mmmm…good stuff." He sat the canteen, still open, next to me and said, "Have a drink." I stared at the canteen, wanting it; yearning for it. It seemed to be a million kilometers away, even though it was only a few centimeters from my hand.

The man stood and walked away, leaving the canteen at my side. The door slammed shut while I continued to stare at the canteen. It became my only concern; nothing else mattered to me at that moment. I knew where the canteen was, but I could not move to save my life.

Using every bit of my energy and strength, I managed to slide my hand to the canteen. I could not, however, get my hand around it, let alone, pick it up. I began to think of ways to get the water to my mouth. After a period of time had passed, I decided that I had to get onto my side and tip the canteen into my mouth.

Without thinking, I used the last of my strength to force myself over. I fell hard against the floor. My head contacted, hard, causing an intense headache. I laid there for several moments. I attempted, several times, to knock the canteen over, failing every time. I was beginning to lose hope, thinking I was too weak.

Hours, it seemed, passed by. I was becoming weaker by the moment and my thirst grew as my tongue began to swell in my mouth. Finally, I managed to knock the canteen over. Feeling victorious, I began to lap, with my tongue, at the floor. It took several moments for me to realize, the canteen had been empty the whole time, causing me to become angered.

I laid there for what seemed to be an eternity before I began to doze off. Slowly, I slipped into a sleep. I did not believe I would awaken from that sleep, for it felt as though I was going to die; I 'knew' that I was going to die. Without a fight, I had given up.

I woke to someone squeezing my ankle again. I could not focus at first, but soon realized the man had returned and I was not dead. I could not see him. I could only hear him talking. I could not focus enough to understand what he was saying. When I did not respond, he squeezed harder. I tried to fight back, but it was of no use; I could not move.

After a few moments, the man stood. I tried to see what he was doing, but failed. I heard him yelling and then heard a loud snapping noise as a sensation of pain, worse than any I had ever felt before, shot up my leg. I tried to scream, but no noise came forth. In a matter of seconds I passed out from the pain.

A loud noise awakened me. I opened my eyes and saw the silhouette of a man in the doorway in the light. I dreaded what was going to happen next. I closed my eyes in hopes he would simply kill me this time. I could hear his footsteps as he neared me. I felt my heart sink more and more the closer he got. Panicking in silence, I began to cry.

Sukata asked, "What happened to you?" This time with a playful tone in his voice along with a rasp as though he was being choked. I opened my eyes as he bent down, grabbed me under the arms, and began to drag me toward the door. I felt relieved, knowing that I was saved.

He dragged me out into another room. The room reminded me of a large ballroom with a balcony wrapped around a large fountain in the center and a court below. I could not see clearly so this was all I could distinguish.

Sukata dragged me to a wall or something similar and propped me against it. He asked, "Are you good? How bad are you fucked up?" I could not reply and instead mumbled as loud as I could. He got the idea and retrieved some water. Like a bird might feed its young, Sukata tilted my head back and slowly poured small amounts of the water into my mouth. I reveled the feeling of the water quenching my thirst as it soothed the raw flesh inside my throat.

Once Sukata felt I had enough to drink, he set the bottle down and began to pull my pant leg up to examine my ankle. I cringed with pain with every touch. Sukata knew it was bad, but he had to do what he needed to. I gritted my teeth and toughed through the pain.

When Sukata saw the damage, he said, "Holy shit! They fucked you up good!" I still could not respond, for my mouth was still quite swollen. He examined my leg with the caution of a mouse searching for food. It seemed only a few seconds had passed before he looked at me. With a strange look on his face, as though he was going to enjoy something, he said, "I have to set it. You're not gonna like it. But, I need you to bear with me. I'll make it quick as possible. One…Two…" He did not count to three.

My leg made an awful grinding and crunching noise as he pulled, twisted, and shifted my leg. I screamed; this time noise expelling from my mouth as my face became hot and scrunched. I nearly passed out from the pain, but fought myself to stay awake. I could hear Sukata counting again,

"One…Two…" Again the intense pain came as he shifted my foot, setting my ankle. I could not bear it and blacked out. Sukata awakened me with more water and promise of food. I opened my eyes to find him holding my head up, tapping my cheek. When he saw that my eyes were open, he stopped tapping and reached down, picking up a bottle of water, saying, "You need to drink. I don't know how long you went without water. I know they found me the day after they took you." 'The day after they took me?' I wondered, 'How long had I been in that room?'

It took a while for me to completely gain consciousness. I felt groggy and disorientated. I did not know where I was or how long it had been since I fell. I only knew that I was in a lot of pain and Sukata was helping me get through it.

Sukata spent nearly the entire day feeding and hydrating me, trying to bring me to health. I tried my best to help, but I was too weak. He understood, and did what he could. He explained to me that he used newspaper and tape, he had found in the mall, to splint my leg and ankle; that it would keep my leg stable but I would not be able to apply weight to it for a couple weeks at earliest.

Eventually, I dozed off. When I awoke, Sukata was gone. I looked around for him. I could not see him nor could I hear him. I began to worry, 'Has he left me? Is he coming back?' I sat there for some time before I dozed off again.

I awoke to Sukata holding a rifle, examining it. He was sitting on a bench that he must have dragged nearer to me. I looked at him for a while and then tried to speak, "Hey." The word came hoarse and little more than a mutter. He turned his head to look at me and put his finger to his mouth and shushed me.

He set the rifle down on the bench and picked up a pistol, pointing it in my direction, yet not at me. I did not know if he was going to shoot me like a horse with a broken leg or if he was simply testing out the pistol. I became worried, but then calmed when I thought about all he had done to save me, 'Why would he kill me now? Why not before he used all that supplies?' I was just overreacting.

Later that day, Sukata explained to me that he had found a .30-06 rifle and a large box of rounds. He showed me the rifle and told me that he would trade it for the .22 rifle I had and that we could talk about it later. He then showed me three pistols he had found and said, "I'll let you have any one you want as long as it's not this one," waving the very large one, "I have plenty of ammo for all of them and I also found a couple cleaning kits for these and the rifles." I looked up at him, I felt too weak to move much; I believe he realized that I could not move and said, "Later."

I was in and out for most of the day. Sukata checked on me periodically; feeding me and giving me water. When night came, Sukata laid me on my side and allowed me to sleep. He explained that by morning I should be able to move a little better and he would help me regain my strength. It only took a few moments for me to fall fast asleep.

It was midday when I awoke again. This time Sukata was changing the bandages on my hand, the ones on my wrists had already been changed. I asked, "What's wrong with my hand?," my voice still quite hoarse. He looked at me and said, "When you get the strength to remove the bandages yourself, you'll know." I stared at him, worried. I tried to raise my hand enough to remove the bandage, but could not. Sukata said, "It may be a few days, but that will give you time to prepare yourself. For now, we need to get you movin.' Otherwise, you're not gonna get your strength back." He offered me his right hand. I accepted and he pulled me up, pulling my arm over his shoulders with his left hand, helping me balance on my left leg. He helped me walk to the bench and let me sit down. Standing there for a moment, making sure I was alright, he said, "Stay put. I'll be right back," as he walked away.

It seemed hours had passed before he returned. He was holding a pair of crutches and said, "I don't know that these will work but it's worth a shot." Handing them to me, he said, "You like whiskey?" I looked up at him as though he had asked a stupid question. "Alright. Well, I found some Scotch in the cigar shop. Cigars too." I looked at him with an expression of expectation on my face. Reaching behind a sign he retrieved a small crate.

He carried the crate over to the bench, set it in front of me, and opened it. Inside there was a box of cigars and six or seven half-liter bottles of Scotch. I became excited and hurried Sukata with a subtle throat-clearing noise. Without hesitation Sukata opened a bottle of the Scotch and poured some into my mouth. The taste was extravagant. It was smooth and relaxingly warm, sliding down my throat as though it were thin, warm milk. I could feel it warm my body as it settled in my stomach.

I felt relaxed and buzzed by the time we finished the first bottle. It did not seem to affect Sukata in the least. I tried to ask him how he did it, but my words were too slurred for him to understand. When he gave me a confused look, I gave up and went to sleep.

I awoke to the smell of eggs and bacon. A refreshing smell it was. I had not had such a pleasure since before the outbreak. I grew anxious with the thought of eating such a treat. The smell entering my nose sent a sensation through my mouth, causing it to water, drowning my taste buds.

When Sukata turned around, I could see him grinning "ear to ear." I knew he was happy to have such a treat also. I said, "Smells wonderful," my voice not nearly as raspy. "That it does, my friend. That it does." He turned back to the small can of fire which he was using to cook.

The meal was quite enjoyable. I loved the texture of the meat. It was not bacon; Sukata said, "Squirrel." I had never had squirrel before but it was a sweet, yet savory meat. I asked, "Where'd you get the eggs?" "They're not real eggs, they're powdered eggs," he explained. I looked at him confused and he handed me a package. I looked it over and then looked at him. "Found 'em in one of the kiosks in the food court," he said. I replied, "Oh, I always wondered what they used."

After we ate, I asked Sukata to tell me what happened. While he talked I examined him; I did not notice that he had several wounds and injuries. His face was blackened with bruises, which were starting to yellow around the edges. His left eye was blood red from exploded veins within his eye. He was missing two teeth. His nose seemed to be broken. And he had a large bruise across his neck with a laceration, centimeters below the bruise.

Sukata explained everything. He told me about the guttering giving way and him making a dive for the ground, combat rolling on impact and then running into a nearby culvert. He told me about watching that man drag me into the mall, shooting those creatures while he did so. In the middle of the story he had to pause, walking away to do something. When he returned, he explained how they found him while he was sleeping and had guns drawn on him so he could not do anything. He explained how he had hidden the small pocket knife in his boot and how they escorted him to the mall.

He went on to tell me how they had beaten him until his eyes had swollen shut, tried to break his fingers but they only dislocated, ripped the nails from some of his fingers, drove nails through his hands, cut his arms and chest with a razor blade, stomped his ribcage until some of his ribs broke, hung him with a cable, and then cut his throat.

It was nearing night before he was done explaining the tortures they had employed. He then went on to explain how he escaped after they cut his throat and left him for dead. "Motherfuckers laid me open good but they're stupid. They cut across not through," he said demonstrating what he meant by dragging his right index finger across his neck then holding it straight as though he were pointing behind himself and moving his right hand from left to right in front of his throat illustrating that they should have pulled the knife through his neck not across. He laughed at the thought of their idiocy. I did not understand what was funny, but continued to listen. When he got himself free, he snuck out and waited until the man went into the room where I was being held. Once the man was inside, he slipped his way over to the woman who was sitting on a bench smoking.

He gave immense details of how he went about cutting her throat the "proper way," "In a single, smooth motion, I grabbed her head, pulled back; I could see her eyes, full of surprise, looking back at me, staring deep into mine, knowing she was about to die, and the last thing she would see is me smiling at her; slid the knife 'through' her neck; I could feel the tip scrape her spine, oh that made me happy; then I ripped her head backward, breaking her neck, listening to the crunch as her spine shattered…just to make sure she was dead. Then I watched the magnificent fountain of blood spray from her jugular as she fell to the ground leaving a massive pool of blood with which she bathed. Aaaw, the glorious sight of death…love it!"

Once he was done, which seemed to take a while (I did not know Sukata could be so poetic nor did I know he had such a passion for killing people), he continued to how he killed the man, "I waited for him to walk out of the room and shanked the shit out of him." He went into further detail, "After I shanked him, I beat him like he beat me, pounding his face in with my bare hands. Then, I stomped his face in until I felt my boot "fall" into his skull. And then stomped his ribcage in

and kicked him to death before he could bleed out on me,"
and then went on to finish the story.

"That's when I found you, nearly dead," completed the tale.
After finishing, he stood and said, "I'll show you around in
the morning." I said, "Alright. Sounds good. But, you never
told me how long I was in that room." He looked at me and
said, "By my guess, I would say it was about four maybe five
days before I found you. I was amazed you were still alive.
They must have been giving you water." "No, they only
played with my mind about the water," I replied. "Did they
pull the canteen trick on you like they did me?" he asked. I
said, "Yeah, how'd you know?" "Because, I told him to eat
shit and kicked it at him, he picked it up, pissed me off and
made me spit my teeth at him and said, 'Maybe your friend'll
want it then.'" I looked at him confused, "What do you mean
he pissed you off and made you spit your teeth at him?" He
grinned and said, "He kicked me in the face, it pissed me off
so I spit my teeth at him."

I wanted to laugh at his cleverness but could not, for my

throat was still a little sore. I, instead, grinned and said,
"Good one." He acknowledged my appreciation of the joke
and walked around the corner of the corridor. He returned a
while later and said, "Wanna sleep in a bed?" Excitedly, I
replied, "Hell yeah!" He walked over to me and helped me
up. We limped toward the shop he had found with beds on
display. I found one that I liked and he left me to find one
that he liked.

The feeling of lying in a bed, for the first time in weeks, was
amazing. It was like lying on a cloud. Every ache in my body
seemed to leave as I relaxed and got comfortable. I could not
believe the pleasures I was enjoying. They seemed so simple
and I had taken them for granted before the outbreak,
something I will never do again.

I will be fast asleep in a matter of seconds.

Log Entry 28

I do not know what happened. I awoke in a strange room somewhere within the mall. I could not see; nor did I know how long I was there. Sukata found me yesterday, informing me that he had been searching for me for three days. All I remember is finishing my journal entry while lying in the bed, soon after passing out, and then awakening in a dark room. I have no idea how I got there; nor do I know what drove me to go to such a place.

Am I going mad? Am I mad? Nothing of these incidents, that I have no memory of, makes sense. I do not understand what is happening. Why do I not remember some of the things that happen to me? How can I simply forget? I must be going mad. There is no other explanation.

Sukata found me yesterday morning. I was too weak to move or write. He aided me once more; this time however, was not as bad as the first. I was simply dehydrated, nothing more. When Sukata opened the door to the room, he casted a light across two dead bodies that had been nearly devoured. I had no idea who they were or where they came from. I was covered in blood, had a strange taste in my mouth, and was not hungry; it felt as though I had eaten a Thanksgiving feast.

Sukata questioned me about the situation and joked at one point; he said, "I didn't think you would become addicted after feeding it to you once." I did not understand until he explained that the "squirrel" was actually human.

I did not believe him; I did not want to believe him. He laughed at me as though I was over reacting; as though it was nothing for him to cannibalize someone. I could not believe how cold he really was and yet he aided me, he protected me, he nursed me to health. Is he keeping me alive in case he needs to eat me? I do not want to think that but, I must.

I may not be able to live with myself knowing that I had consumed human flesh. If it becomes too much to bear, I will have to finish myself and Sukata; for he is the one who had forced such an abomination upon me by feeding me the flesh of his victims.

I cannot grasp why someone would do such a thing. Sukata is

a sick individual; mental and unpredictable. He must have been in an asylum before the outbreak; no 'human' would be able to do such, therefore, he must not be human.

I will keep an eye on Sukata from now on. I will no longer be able to trust him. He may turn on me at any moment and I want to be prepared to fight as best I can. Sukata does not seem like the type to murder unless he has a reason, but hunger seems to be enough for him to do strange things. I am not implying that Sukata will murder me if he is simply hungry, but he may if he is starving.

I am still too weak to write much more. I will stop here for now. I shall return to my journal tomorrow night.

Log Entry 29

I fell asleep without realizing it last night. When I awoke, Sukata was packing our bags. I did not know why; nor did I know what had happened while I slept. I checked myself for any new wounds, finding none. Relieved, I sat up and asked Sukata what he was doing. He explained to me that he was packing our bags because we had to leave today.

I noticed that, when I speak to Sukata, there is hatred in my voice. I do not think Sukata has discovered it yet and I do not care if he does. He may sense it and yet ignore it thinking it is simply my anger for him feeding me human flesh but I may never know.

Sukata acts as though our relationship remains the same; he my mentor, I his pupil. I do feel this is true; then again, I always despised my instructors. I feel Sukata has become more of an authority figure instead of a friend. I do not understand how he can remain so calm in almost every situation we have endured.

I believe I am going mad. I have heard voices and yet see no one from which they come. I have searched every time I hear a voice, finding nothing more than an empty shell of a building. Sukata must recognize my madness, for he continually tells me, "You'll get used to it eventually…or break from it, depends on how strong your mind is." I did not understand what he was speaking of when he first told me, but soon realized when he became sincere.

I find myself becoming more hateful toward Sukata with every passing moment. It seems as though he is my arch nemesis; my ultimate challenge. I do not understand why I have these feelings; surely it is not only because he fed me human, there must be another reason.

My mind has wandered several times. Sukata finds me staring off in the distance at a wall nearly continuously. He simply waves his hand in front of my face and asks, "You alright?" I usually nod, assuring him that I am, and he continues on his way. Soon after, I am lost, once again, in my thoughts of blankness.

Sukata began to explain to me that he had gone through the

very same situation when he was young. I only heard bits and pieces of it as I passed in and out of alertness. He tried several times to comfort me, telling me, "It'll end soon, then you will be fine...not yourself...but fine." I had no idea what he meant by that. He explained it as though it were a drug streaming through my veins causing my mind to stray and when it took its course, I would be reborn as a new person. Sukata is mad. I realize this for sure now. Earlier, he was sitting on a bench near the edge of the balcony, watching the creatures through the front door; he turned to me and said, "I wonder what they taste like." I began to sweat and gave him an evil look. He turned away from me, back to the creatures, and said, "I bet they would taste funny...I guess we'll never find out...I may, you won't though...if I tried to feed you some, you'd probably try to kill me." He broke out in laughter as he finished his statement.

I felt something change in me as I listened to his laugh. It felt like someone had crushed my heart, causing me to break out into a heavier, cold sweat; I began to shiver as though it were cold. Sukata did not turn to look at me for some time. I watched him, my hatred growing as I thought of several ways to kill him.

The sweat began to pour down my face. It felt as though droplets of ice were gliding across my skin as they slid to my jaw line. My heart began to race and my breathing became heavy. I could feel my fingers, toes, and face begin to tingle and then they went numb. My eyes felt as though they were being sucked into the back of my skull as everything seemed to move further and further away, leaving me in the far distance.

I tried to reach for the sign next to the bench I was sitting on and it felt as though it were kilometers away. My breathing became ragged and then blackness.

I awoke in the bed again. Sukata had a bottle of water in his hand, ready for me to awaken. I sat up quickly, Sukata warned against doing such and told me to lie down and take it slow. I did not want to listen to him but soon realized he was correct when my vision began to blur.

After lying in place for a while, I sat up slowly. Sukata was at my side the entire time. I felt a twinge of hatred flow through my body when I saw his face. I could not bring myself to look at him. He stood, set the bottle of water down and walked away. I knew he knew that I hated him. He must not have cared, for he did not say so.

It was after dinner when Sukata explained his plan. When he finished he looked me in the eye and said, "I know what you're feeling, I've been through it. I understand, but remember this: Without me, you would have been dead long ago." He was right, but that did not stop me from feeling what I did. All I know now is that I hate the very man I depend on.

Log Entry 30

We are stopping only to rest for a little while. We have been traveling for two days now.

We escaped the mall through a series of corridors, designed for maintenance, within the walls. When we finally reached the door that led us outside, we were surprised to find that the door was open. We did not waste any time wondering about it and ran like wild rabbits from a crew of dogs. We did not slow to a walk for nearly a kilometer.

Sukata did not wait on me when I fell behind; nor did he speak much throughout our journey. We continued to walk southeast toward the military base that may or may not exist. I can tell Sukata is not at all pleased with the idea of backtracking his path, let alone heading toward a military base; I know this because he stated, "Military bases are death camps in situations like this. They're all stupid. They believe they can 'cure' the infected and protect the people. Why? Because, they have firepower and the number of force? I don't give a fuck what they think they have; they don't have the knowhow nor the mindset to deal with shit like this," while we were walking; he had such hatred in his voice as though I were speaking about him.

I watched Sukata during the entire trip to our current location. I despise him more with every passing moment. I can barely stand to hear his voice. I can barely stand the sight of him. I 'hate' him. I, both, want him to die and yet hope my hatred passes before I kill him, for I 'need' him to survive.

Sukata is cooking as I write, when he is done, we are to eat and continue moving. I will continue my logs as soon as possible.

Log Entry 31

We stopped last night at a small farm house. Sukata

explained that he intends only to stay for a day, allowing our

feet to rest and for us to regain strength. We did not sleep last

night as we were too busy trying to secure the house. When

we finished, we settled in and tried to sleep.

Sukata said that first light tomorrow, we are to start traveling

again. He explained that this is the last stop until we reach

the military base which is approximately (by his calculations)

a week's travel. I do not like the idea of not being able to rest

for an entire week, but we have no other option.

Sukata told me that I am lucky he is even considering helping

me reach the military base. I explained to him the

possibilities it may hold. He did not take a fondness in any of

my thoughts, instead he stared at me until I was done and

then replied, "You are just like the rest of them, you have no

idea what you are getting yourself into and are walking

blindly with false hopes into something you will regret until

you die." That statement drove me to hate him even more. I

feel he does not know what he is talking about nor does he know what is in store for us; yet he speaks as though he has been through such situations a million times.

I did not speak to Sukata for several hours after our short conversation. I could not bring myself to hear his voice without attempting to murder him. I have taken several measures to ensure that I do not attempt such foolish feats, for I am in no condition to do so.

I have tried several times to sleep, failing every time. I feel as though I am in constant danger. Because of this, Sukata has become an obsession. I cannot sleep without wondering if he is somewhere near, ready to kill me or carve me up while I am still alive. I watch his every move as though it were a threat to my own well-being. I have come to hate Sukata with a passion; despise him. He is my nemesis and I his victim awaiting death.

Log Entry 32

We are holding up in a small house near the location of the
military base. It took us nearly ten days to reach our current
location. We arrived late at night and are unable to continue
due to exhaustion. Thus, we have yet to discover whether it
exists or not yet. We intend to scout it at first light.

It has been nearly nine days since the last time I slept. My
body is so exhausted that I no longer have the ability to stand
with any stability. My mind is so exhausted that
concentration is nearly impossible; it has taken nearly an
hour to write thus far. It seems as though Sukata is unaffected
by the lack of sleep and nutrition; providing more evidence
for my former theory of him being inhuman.

Sukata has become my absolute obsession. I follow his every
move. It is as though I am a starving frog following a fly with
eyes that seem to have the ability to devour the creature
without the aid of the mouth. With every twitch, every move
he makes, my eyes instantly lock onto him. I do not believe
that I will be able to sleep even now.

To help myself stay awake, I will write about our journey. I will start from the mall and fill in the blanks between my logs. Not all of the journey will be recorded due to the inability to focus clearly and forgetting segments. I will, however, attempt to record every event as accurately as possible.

Once we escaped the mall, we ran as fast as we could (I much slower than Sukata). Sukata did not wait for me to catch up at any point and instead would only stop when he needed to get a drink, fix something, or kill some creatures he had run into. I continued as fast as I could, trying my best to keep up with Sukata. I managed to meet him several times, however, was soon left behind as Sukata would continue on. It was nearly the end of the first day, when we encountered a forest; through which Sukata planned to travel. This slowed me down more. Due to the soft and broken ground, I was unable to securely plant the crutches, which hindered my movement. Sukata, however, seemed to walk through it as though it were no different than walking across a flat, paved highway.

I did not meet any creatures along our journey, for Sukata had destroyed most every one of them that fell into his path. I would encounter the remains and gore that he left behind. Several times, I discovered intestines and other organs strewn through trees and smashed heads splattered across the ground, covering the area with massive amounts of blood and brain. I would try to avoid these scenes as much as possible for they made me nauseous.

By the end of the second day we reached the edge of the forest. We stopped soon after, near a traffic tunnel. Sukata thought it to be stupid to do such but, we had to either traverse the tunnel or continue around the tunnel which may have added two to three days to our journey. Since Sukata opted to avoid adding any more time than needed, he decided that we needed to stop and rest before attempting to forge a path through the tunnel.

After resting, for a moment, eating and drinking some water, we continued on into the tunnel. At first, we were unable to see but a few feet in front of us. Eventually, it became so dark that I could not see my hand in front of my face. Sukata told me to keep close and pulled a flashlight form his bag.

We continued through the tunnel until we spotted something moving ahead, and a massive pile of vehicles blocked our path.

Sukata prepared for a fight, assuming that the movement had to be one of those creatures. We discovered soon enough, that he was right but, we did not expect there to be several of them. The creatures were trapped in the vehicles, their arms flailing wildly as though they were trying to reach us. Their mouths were chomping, snarling, lashing out, as though they were trying to bite us from a distance.

The only way to make progress was to climb over the pile of vehicles. The creatures inside the vehicles, because we did not know where they were, proved to make the task much more difficult and extremely dangerous. Sukata took the lead, watching his every move as though he were climbing the side of a cliff without any safety gear; fearing he would make a mistake which would cause him to fall to his death.

Sukata began climbing on a section of the vehicles that had very few openings and tried to avoid any area that a creature may be able to reach out of. Once he reached the midpoint, I began to climb myself, working from side to side, using my right knee instead of causing more damage to my broken ankle. It was a hard and painful climb. When Sukata reached the top, he began to spot me, helping me through the gauntlet of openings that creatures could have been in.

Once I reached the midpoint myself, a hand jutted from one of the car doors, grabbing my left wrist with the grip of a vise. I attempted, failing, to free myself from the grasp of the creature that held me. Sukata kept yelling instructions on how to work my wrist free. I tried every one, failing. Sukata did not climb down to help me but instead, turned away from me and scouted the other side of the pile.

Finally, I freed my hand by stabbing the creature with the crutch in my right hand. Once free, I heard something behind me and turned to see what created the noise. There were several creatures making their way to us. I scurried the rest of the way to the top of the mound as fast as I could. Sukata aided me to the top and we continued on.

I began to yell at Sukata, "Why didn't you help me?!" He just stared at me as though it were a stupid question and continued to walk. I asked again more calmly, "Why didn't you help me?" He turned to look at me and shined the flashlight in my face. "I didn't help you because that puts us both in danger and besides, you had it under control," he explained. I became angrier at the thought of Sukata leaving me to die. We made it out of the tunnel just before night. Sukata did not stop and continued as before. I fell behind within a few minutes and was not able to catch up. I knew that Sukata did not care and felt that I was only slowing him down. I grew to hate him even more for he did not do anything to aid me, even if he were to simply leave me behind to die.

The terrain was harsh due to the destruction caused by the military, the police, and the anarchy that swept over the population. Avoiding the highway as much as possible and yet staying close enough to provide a means of navigation, we slowly made progress through the tree ridden valleys. The hills that the valleys lay between caused us to slow to a crawl when climbing them. Despite this, we traveled as hastily as possible with few breaks; not stopping for more than a minute or two. Sukata avoided any areas that seemed to be difficult for me to traverse. I commended him for his consideration but, still, my hatred continued to grow as we walked.

Throughout that night and the following day, we did not encounter anymore creatures until approximately midnight the following night. Breaking through the edge of a large patch of trees, landing us near the highway, we happed across a large factory of sorts. Thinking that we would be able to find some sort of supplies if we were careful, and I stayed outside keeping watch, Sukata decided to investigate. I thought this was a good idea because we were running low on water. We only had approximately eight liters left which would only last us another two to three days.

Using the same technique Sukata had several other times, he tested the building. Once he felt it was safe, he entered, leaving the door open to ensure I would be able to signal him, if needed. He explained that he would not be long and he would only explore the areas that were most likely to contain water or food. I felt comfortable with that, thinking that it would only be a few moments before he returned. I felt that he should have been able to make quick work of the search and that I would not have to worry about any creatures within that short time span.

When Sukata disappeared into the building, I felt relieved, somewhat, at the idea of him being gone. It felt as though the hatred that I harbored had subsided for the moment and I could concentrate on something other than Sukata. This made me feel much better about the situation and made for a few decent moments in which I relaxed, nearly passing out.

Nearly asleep, I heard something within the building.

Thinking it was Sukata returning, I walked to the doorway to see what he had found. As I stepped into view of the corridor on the other side of the door, I became sick to my stomach. At the opposite end of the corridor, there stood several of those creatures, most of which were wearing name tags and hard hats; thus, making me believe that they were the workers of the factory.

Quickly reacting, I slammed the door, sat down in front of it, pushing against it as hard as I could. I could hear the creatures nearing the door as their coughing and growling became louder. My heart began to race when I felt them press against the door, causing my breathing to become ragged. I knew that I was going to die if Sukata did not return soon. I could not fight them all off myself and would not be able to hold them off for very long. I readied myself with my glaive and hoped that I would not have to battle in my condition. It seemed like an eternity had passed while I was trying to hold the door shut; the creatures' fingers breaking through the small gap in the door when they would shove against it; forcing me forward slightly. When their fingers wrapped around the door, I swung my glaive, sliding the blade along the edge of the door, severing the fingers from the hands that they were attached to, as though they were cobs of corn being reaped from the stalk, causing them to fall the ground as though they were small, bloody sausages that had been mauled. This did not seem to faze the creatures, for they did not hesitate, continuing to push the door harder.

I was becoming quite tired and weak, wanting to discontinue my efforts and let my fate come to be. Feeling as though another eternity had passed, I began to consider death as an option. I felt that it would be more of a relief at that point and began to give in. I knew that I would be torn limb from limb like a bug in a cruel child's hands; plucked apart as though my limbs were removable; sundered as though my body were made of tissue paper; dying as my insides are ripped out and strewn across the ground as though I were being mauled by several bears that were searching through a, strangely shaped, box for something near the bottom.

I was beginning to let the door open more, when suddenly the creatures stopped. Surprised and relieved at the same time, I prepared myself for them to burst through the door as though they were relay racers crossing the finish line with a massive explosion of energy. When nothing happened, I became curious. I slowly got to my feet and awaited something to happen.

Suddenly, something pushed against the door hard. I again applied pressure to the door trying to keep it shut. A second time something hit the door, I applied more pressure. Then something began to beat on the door; I did not budge. I set my ear to the door, listening. Sukata was in the other side yelling and cussing. Relieved to hear him and yet dreading his presence, I stepped away from the door.

Sukata pushed the door open, revealing himself. Covered in blood, his clothes torn and the machete in his right hand dripping blood as though it were a faucet of sorts, he stepped out of the building. With anger in his voice, he said, "What the fuck?! What the fuck is wrong with you? I was trying to open the damn door. I just killed probably six or seven of those damn things and you're out here being stupid, holding the fucking door shut while I'm beating on it." I became angered, making my hatred for Sukata become more intense. "I thought you were one of them!" I screamed. "I have never seen, nor heard, one of those damn things beat on a door while yelling. They don't speak!" he yelled. I stood there for a moment, trying to keep calm, and then yelled, "I didn't fucking hear you!"

Sukata did not reply to that last statement and instead turned away and dropped his bag next to the building and dropped his machete on the ground. Confused, I stood where I was and watched. Sukata began searching through his bag, using only his right hand. After a few moments, he retrieved a blanket and some cordage; I continued to watch.

He, carefully, wrapped the blanket around his left arm, pulling it tight as he wrapped it. Once he had the blanket wrapped, several times, around his arm, using the entire length, he began wrapping the cordage around it, securing it to his arm. Once he reached the end of the cordage, he tucked the end under a few of the wraps and tied a strange knot in it. Still confused, I continued to watch.

Once he had finished, he put is bag on his back once more, grabbed his machete and began to walk again. I hurried to follow him, being careful not to get too close. I could see Sukata limping, making me think he must have been injured somehow.

With his left arm injured badly (I believe broken), and his right leg badly injured, Sukata still acted as though it did not faze him; as though it were normal; nothing to worry about; just a scratch or bruise. I became increasingly worried, thinking Sukata had been bitten. Since he did not say anything, I did not know. He simply walked in silence as though I did not exist.

I began to hate Sukata more for not setting me at ease, holding me on edge, knowing that if he were bitten, it would make for a very difficult situation when he began to act like one of those creatures. Sukata seems like the type to shoot himself if he were bitten though, so I do not understand. If he was bitten he would have shot himself already. This allowed for a little peace of mind but did not let my mind rest.

We continued traveling; Sukata had slowed to nearly my pace for his limp slowed him greatly. With every step, he acted as though his leg was going to break, forcing him to step lightly. Because of this, when Sukata would stop for a drink of water, I was able to catch up easily.

Even with Sukata being badly injured, we continued to travel off road, avoiding any area that may have had a population. Despite this, we had nearly two days of easy travel, seeing only one or two of those creatures, every so often. Sukata made easy work of them for the most part but, sometimes dodged one and made me deal with it. This made me hate him more.

Our journey became harder on the fifth day, for I began to fall asleep walking, causing me to wander off in different directions or collapse. Sukata never helped me; he simply watched over me until I awoke (if I collapsed) or redirected me (if I wandered off). I was not actually sleeping, for I was still conscious of everything around me but, I was unable to control my body. It was a strange feeling. I was still moving, in some cases, and still had the ability to hold a conversation; I just could not direct my body; nor could I grip things or keep my balance.

Sukata knew that I was weak and exhausted, but he never once aided me. He continuously repeated, "You're slowing me down" or "Don't make me kill you," or "Come on, you pansy, get up, we gotta keep movin'." Never once did he stop and help me to my feet or help me stay awake. I felt like I was a slave that did not have to work, just walk.

Fortunately, for us, we did not encounter any creatures on the fifth day. Sukata kept speaking to himself about how that paranoid him and that we must be further into the country than he thought. I do not know if that was a bad thing or not but, he seemed unconcerned and continued on.

By the sixth day, I was near death; it seemed. Sukata, finally, let me take a break and allowed me to eat something. He began to ask questions again but this time they seemed to be more focused and I understood why he asked them. He asked things like: "Wanna talk about it?" or "You can hate me all you want, I've done enough for you and I'm not your father...is that what you want me to be?" or "Have I pissed you off yet?" He didn't have to ask the questions; he already knew the answers; he just wanted to teach me a lesson in reality; he wanted to teach me that I could not depend on him forever and that I would have to learn to solve my own problems.

The seventh day came upon us with a downpour of rain. Sukata and I both were soaked. Sukata didn't seem to mind until his feet became wet from water seeping into his boots. We did not stop even then; continuing like soldiers with a single goal; as though we were brainwashed, mindless, or cyborgs searching for something our masters sent us after. The rain became so heavy at one point that we were unable to see ahead of us. Sukata seemed to be concerned, but not weary of the situation. Instead of getting excited, Sukata simply held his machete out, with his right hand, as though it were a lance, moved his back pack to the front of him, and tucked his left arm between him and the bag. I was confused by his technique until we encountered a few creatures.

Due to Sukata's inability to see, he waited for a creature to charge him, if the creature missed the machete, he would sort of duck behind his bag as he retracted his arm, using the bag as a shield and then begin stabbing and slashing at the creature; this reminded me of the technique a Spartan would use while in a Phalanx formation. Amazed by his ingenuity, I did the same in hope that it would enhance my chances of survival.

I failed to use the technique properly, for I could not use my right leg; I was forced to the ground by a creature that had flanked me from my left, twisting my right ankle, causing intense pain to shoot up my leg. Scared and trying to keep from passing out, I did all that I could to keep awake while fighting the creature off.

Sukata did not intervene any more than he needed to, to prevent the creature from biting me. He made me figure it out on my own. I was nearly bitten several times. I struggled with the creature until one the glass shanks punctured my bag, stabbing the creature in the left eye as I rolled over, in turn shoving it deep into its skull. This caused a massive gush of blood to expel from the creature's eye socket, covering my bag with infected blood.

Relieved that I was still alive, I laid there, breathing heavy and relaxed for a moment. Sukata did not wait, did not say anything, did not help me to my feet; he simply walked away as though we never stopped. I felt a hard twinge of hatred flood my chest. My mind began to burn with the hatred, which it contained, for Sukata.

Eight days into our trip, we encountered a group of soldiers (Sukata had used the scope on his rifle to scout when he spotted them). They did not see us, for we were hidden within the trees well, but we could see them well enough. Sukata estimated them to be approximately five kilometers ahead of us. They had established a road block on the highway. From Sukata's description, there were four posted on the top of a personnel transport vehicle, three on the ground under the personnel transport vehicle, two on each end of the road block, two inside the vehicle, and four in each of the Humvees at either end of the road block.

I wanted to get to them as quickly as possible, thinking they would help us. Sukata advised against doing such, explaining that they will simply "shoot us and loot us." I tried to coax him into at least investigating further but he was having none of that. Instead, he zeroed in with my .22 rifle, using great care, and fired at them. After he fired he looked through his scope to see which, if any, he hit. On the first shot he reported, "Got one…now they're running around like cockroaches when you turn the lights on."

My hatred grew to the extent of wanting nothing more than to rip Sukata's face from his skull and watch as he drowned in a puddle of his own blood. I was careful not to show any signs of hatred and bit my tongue, for I was in no condition to travel alone.

On the second shot, Sukata began to cuss because he missed.

I, again, tried to talk him into investigating further. He did not look at me but replied, "Go then. Go to your heroes if that's what you wanna do. If they don't shoot you, then I will admit that you were right." He fired another round; this time injuring one of the men in the personnel transport vehicle (Sukata said, "Dumb fuck will have the window up the next time.")

Sukata sent six more rounds down range before he stopped and said, "We gotta move." Confused, I just stared at him. He turned to find me gawking at him as though he were some strange creature. He just shook his head, got up, and started walking. I quickly followed, even though I wanted to shoot him.

We strayed from the highway (Sukata feared we would be spotted) and instead moved deeper into the forest. As we traveled, I became leery of Sukata, for he seems to have the ability to kill people without any conscious afterthought. This seems to be from the lack of a guilty conscience which may very well prove to be my end if I do not keep myself in check. I may never understand Sukata but, I believe he may have grown up in a world far different than my own.

The sun of the ninth morning was gorgeous. We had a clear view of it as we walked along the highway, carefully listening. Sukata did not appreciate having to entertain the idea of walking along the highway but we had no other choice, for that was our only way to cross the massive river ahead.

I loved the feeling of the solid, smoothed ground beneath my feet; it gave me a sense of security. Sukata, however, seemed to become less secure, the longer we stayed on the highway. He would continuously read the map and count paces as though he hoped the river would have moved closer so that we would not have to travel much further on the highway.

I did not understand it but, Sukata acted as though he were a fugitive or a refugee trying to avoid detection. With every meter we walked he seemed to become more and more anxious to reach the bridge. It may have been due to his hatred for authority figures or possibly just that he did not want to deal with people.

Nearly a kilometer away from the bridge, Sukata stopped. I became worried, thinking he had spotted something of significant danger. When he, suddenly, ran to the opposing side of the road, I was startled. As I walked toward him, I spotted the trail of blood that he had left on the ground. Worried about what may have caused the wound that left the trail and not about Sukata, I ran toward him.

When he turned to look at me, I could see him attempting to pull an arrow from his shoulder. I was both happy and dreadful. I did not know what would become of us. I feared we would die here on the highway. Sukata told me to grab the arrow and shove it through his shoulder. I was confused but gladly obliged. Grabbing the arrow in my hands, I felt as though I had control of Sukata; I felt that he relied on me for that one moment.

I gripped the arrow with all of my strength and shoved as hard as I could, forcing the arrow through Sukata's shoulder. The arrow shot through the backside of his shoulder blade as though it were a large, slow moving bullet. Blood splattered everywhere as the skin burst open. Sukata let out a grunt of pain and reached behind himself, grabbed the arrow and pulled it through the rest of the way. I watched in awe as blood began to pour from his shoulder.

Sukata did not react as I expected; he was much calmer than I would have been. Maintaining self-control, Sukata ripped the bottom of his shirt into strips and began stuffing them into the wound on either side. Once he finished, he tore the remaining part of his shirt into strips and wrapped his shoulder tightly. I was amazed by his sheer tolerance of pain and watched as he quickly bandaged himself and raised his rifle to the injured shoulder searching for the source.

I believed Sukata would have searched for the culprit but, I think his mind was not together that day. I did not discover until later, that he knew the person that had shot him; thus, he was not worried about it. Not knowing this I was still in shock and was highly curious as to why so many people wanted Sukata dead. I did not ask questions and instead allowed Sukata to explain as he felt necessary. "That bitch, I thought she was dead! GRr I can't believe she actually shot me! I'll…ah fuck it, she'll be dead soon enough," Sukata said under his breath as he looked through his scope.

I did not understand why a second or third arrow was not fired. I was curious as to why someone would attempt to kill someone but when they failed, simply run away. That's when I heard a vehicle with a diesel engine and I turned to look down the highway. Sukata must have heard it before me, because as I turned back, he was gone. I did not hesitate and ran into the brush, disappearing as quickly as possible.

Once I felt I was hidden, I turned back to the highway to watch the vehicle pass. There were three of them. One large truck and two Hummer type vehicles. I did not realize it at first but, the large truck was the personnel transport vehicle and the Hummers were actually Humvees. They were the vehicles Sukata was shooting at earlier.

Every nerve in my body told me to run out and flag them down but Sukata's words held strong and I halted myself. I did not want to believe Sukata was right but, I had a feeling that he was. I would not be certain of this until later that day. Once the vehicles passed, I sighed. Sukata startled me, saying, "Glad you didn't run out there when you realized who it was. I didn't want to gunfight with a machete and a .22." I had not realized that he had walked up next to me and squatted down. He seemed to be joking but, with a hint of seriousness within his voice.

We waited to be sure that the vehicles were out of hearing range before we moved. Sukata told me to take it easy and take my time because they may be waiting down the road. I heeded his words for they may have saved my life.

As we approached the highway again, we heard a series of popping noises off in the distance. We paid no mind to them, even though Sukata said, "Sounds like gunshots…maybe they got that bitch." I knew that he was probably right; they, most likely, were gunshots. I did not want to believe they were because that would prove Sukata right about the military; something that I dreaded the thought of; the military being corrupt.

No more than a kilometer from our hiding position, we found three bodies. All of them were completely stripped and each had three to four bullet holes in its chest. Sukata did not say anything; he just looked at me with an expression that explained it well enough. He was right.

After examining the bodies more closely, we noticed that the woman had been raped or, at least, had extremely rough intercourse; either of which would have caused the same amount of trauma. Sukata seemed to know that it was rape; he seemed to become filled with hatred directed toward the men that did this; as I did toward him. His hatred for those men seemed to be as intense as, or more intense than, the hatred I hold for him.

Sukata seemed to be filled with adrenaline as he walked; faster than before, down the highway in the direction of the vehicles had gone. He walked so fast that we reached the bridge just after midday. Crossing it seemed to be a challenge, for the plates that covered the surface of the bridge were slippery with oil or some type of fuel. Sukata said that it smelled similar to napalm and figured that it was a safety precaution. He explained that since the bridge is built of concrete and steel, the napalm would only do minor damage to the structure but would be devastating to anything crossing the bridge. I did not understand how they would have lit the napalm; until Sukata found a trip line in the center of the bridge.

We used a side railing to pass over the trip line instead of trying to step over it. Sukata believed that he found the ignition source that would have been triggered given the trip line worked; it was a rat trap that had a hole drilled in the center near the front, which a shotgun shell that had been packed with an explosive target load (Tannerite) had been inserted, and the metal wire had a sharpened roofing nail wired in place, aiming at the primer of the shotgun shell. Sukata disassembled the rig and lowered the wire on the rat trap, after removing the shotgun shell. He explained that we can use it at a later time. I did not see the potential of such a device but Sukata is quite ingenious; a regular MacGyver. I had faith that he would be able to come up with something when the time came.

It was near dusk when Sukata spotted the vehicles through his scope. They were camping out in the house that we are in now. Sukata scoped the area out and came to the conclusion that there were seventeen still remaining, two of them injured, one of the injured near death. As Sukata scoped them out, he mapped their positions in the dirt. Twelve of them were outside, while the rest were inside the house. They had a large fire but, did not seem to have any reason for the house other than to sleep in.

Sukata had me hide in a culvert nearby, on the right side of the road when facing the house, and made his way to a large barn, that was near falling, on the opposing side of the road. From there, he would be able to see most of the men outside but, would not have a clear view of the house or its occupants.

I watched the barn, seeing small flashes of light and hearing popping noises, as he fired toward the men. He did not fire at a fast rate; he shot one round at a time, confirmed a hit, and then fired another. Each time I could hear the men yelling about someone being shot or screaming in pain.

It was not long before the remaining men ran for cover in the house. Once the last man left Sukata's field of view, he returned to my position, informing me that there were only seven or eight left. I commended Sukata for his marksmanship as he began to sneak toward the house, using the brush alongside the road for cover.

Moments after Sukata left, I began to hear a series of pops with periods of silence in between. I did not know if Sukata was reloading or moving to a new position. I could only see the fire and the house from my position so, I kept count of the men that went down, whether dead or just injured.

Once Sukata had taken out most of them, he moved closer to the house, using the vehicles as cover; crawling underneath them. I believe Sukata had planned to enter the house and clear it the rest of the way but, instead, began to pull things loose from beneath the vehicles and throwing them on the fire. I was confused by his actions until the fire began to pop like the .22 rifle did when Sukata fired it.

His plan worked well; the remaining men began to shoot in the direction of the fire, revealing their positions. Sukata fired another series of rounds and the night went silent. I could not see any movement nor could I see Sukata any longer, so I sat still.

Moments later, the silence was broken by a series of louder pops; I feared the worst. I knew that the shots fired were not from the .22 rifle but, instead, from one of the soldiers' rifles. I felt relieved and yet sick. My hatred had subsided because the source of it was dead, or so I thought, and yet sick because without him I was sure to die. I did not know what to do or how to react.

When Sukata appeared, holding his left arm with his right hand and the .22 rifle, a larger rifle, and his .50 rifle slung over his left shoulder, I became angry and yet relieved (this time for my own sake). I did not know what had happened;

nor did I know why he was holding his arm but I did not care. He was alive which, both, pissed me off and made me happy.

When Sukata reached me, he explained that the house was clear and that we needed to get inside before any creatures show up for the feast because of the noise. I agreed and followed him. Once we reached the house, Sukata examined his wound, saying, "Clean through. Alright!" I assumed that he meant it to be a good thing but, I do not know.

Sukata bandaged his arm and began dragging bodies out to the fire. I sat down and began to write. I knew that Sukata did not like me sitting down right then, but I also knew that he knew that I would have been of no use to him. So instead of aiding him, he instructed me to cook and threw four M.R.E.s at me. I did as I was told and walked outside to the fire.

Once I finished cooking, and Sukata and I finished eating, he began to throw the bodies onto the fire and told me I needed to cover him in case something came along. I did as I was told, once again, and when he finished, we entered the house at nearly dawn.

We were both so tired that we could barely move so, we went our separate ways to rest. I sat near the front living area in a chair, while Sukata went toward the back of the house. I did not hear from Sukata until nearly midday, when he entered the front area of the house and began telling me about another girl that the soldiers had brought back with them and how he had simply put her out of her misery instead of doing more harm.

The thought of the soldiers keeping a woman, intending only to rape her repeatedly made me sick. The thought of Sukata killing her because of that also made me sick. I hate those soldiers as much as I hate Sukata now. They got what they deserved, if not, they got off easy.

Sukata has now passed out so, I will go to sleep myself. I can only hope that I get enough rest before we travel again. And, I can only hope, that we don't travel as we just did any more, for my body will not be able to endure it.

Log Entry 33

We did not scout today, for we had to secure the small house to prevent the creatures from gaining access. Sukata believes that we will be using this as our "home base" for a few days while we scout the military base, if it exists, since it is close enough for us to travel to and from. He explained that if the base is too far we will find a different place but, if we do not secure this location, it may be over ran if we return.

Sukata approached me with a strange expression on his face. The look seemed to be one of thought and consideration. I simply stared at him while he stood in silence. I did not seem to have the same hatred at the moment; instead, it was a feeling more along the lines of concern.

Several moments passed before Sukata said anything. When he did speak, he had a tone of confusion and yet disappointment. He said, "I've spent most of the day thinking about this...trying to remember...wondering if I am correct...I have come to the conclusion that I am, in fact, correct...Those men I killed last night weren't military...well two of them were…the rest weren't though…I didn't realize it until just a few moments ago but the bodies were all wrong." I stared at him with confusion and asked, "What do you mean?" He looked at the floor toward his boots and then replied, "The boots…the boots were wrong...the military uses combat boots, whether they're black, tan, brown, green, it doesn't matter. But those men were wearing random work boots…except those two…but that isn't what gave it away…it was the way they wore their pants. Soldiers 'always' tuck their pants inside their boots. 'Always.' Only the two wore their pants tucked in like that. The rest wore their pants as though they were civilians…This brought about other thoughts…their uniforms were filled with bullet holes and the badges were entirely wrong…none of them were in the right place." I continued to stare at him with confusion. He continued, "That means that the men I killed were civilians 'not' soldiers, well, with the exception of those two…that explains why they were such bad shots." When Sukata looked up at me, I was still staring at him in confusion. I asked, "How did you figure all that and how do you know they were bad shots?" He looked at me and said, "It's the only way that makes sense," he raised his shirt, "and they fired shit loads of rounds and only hit me once." There was a bullet hole in Sukata's side. I began to become worried. Sukata explained that it didn't hit anything vital but it hurt like hell and he didn't notice it until his adrenaline ran out. He showed me both sides and explained that the bullet had traveled just below the surface; thus, missing his kidney.

Once Sukata was done explaining everything, he told me that I should find a pair of boots that fit from the pile of items he took off the bodies. I was leery about wearing a dead man's boots, for I was always told, "Don't wear the boots of a dead man unless you intend to end up in his place." Thinking about that, I looked at my boots. Realizing that they would not hold up much longer, I walked to the pile which was located in the center of the front yard, near the trucks. I dug through the pile trying every boot that I could find against my boot.

Eventually, I found a pair that should fit well and took my boots off. When I pulled my right boot off, the smell of infection flooded the air and pain began to shoot up my leg. I did not worry about the left boot at that moment and instead peeled the sock from my right foot. The wound had healed over in most places. Where it had not healed over, there was a yellowish liquid oozing from the openings. The flesh of my foot was extremely raw and I could not bear to touch it.

I waited for several moments before I tried to take my left boot off. When I took the sock off, the flesh, like my right foot, was raw. I let my feet dry for a while before trying to put the "new" boot on my left foot. It fit, but was uncomfortable. I believe that it will feel better once they are broken in to my feet.

I got to my feet and walked back into the house carrying the other boot. Luckily the crutches allowed me to keep my right foot from touching the ground. The pain, that every breeze caused, was intense.

Once inside, I sat down and cleaned the wound as best I

could. When I finished, I removed my left boot again and allowed my feet to dry further. Sukata felt that he should do the same since we were not traveling today and took his boots off.

While we sat in the living area quietly, Sukata examined his wounds, cleaned them, and bandaged them. His leg was not broken but it was severely bruised and his knee had been twisted nearly all the way around. His right shoulder (the one that was hit with the arrow) was extremely tender, causing Sukata to grunt with every touch. His left arm was badly bruised and seemed to be fractured. He explained that it was not broken because he could not bend his arm between joints (he literally tried to fold his arm).

When he finished cleaning and bandaging his wounds, Sukata walked around the small house collecting supplies. I continued to let my feet dry and began writing. Sukata is now expecting help, so I will end it here for now.

Log Entry 34

Sukata and I took an inventory of our equipment in preparation of a scouting mission we have planned. Sukata plans to leave just before night and hopes to reach the military base at approximately first light.

In our equipment count, we have: four M4 Carbines (two of which have damaged magazine wells due to gunfire produced by Sukata and one of which is missing the bolt), two AR15 5.56 NATO (one of which the barrel is demolished), three nine millimeter pistols (one of which is packed full of dirt and incapable of fire), two .22 revolvers (one of which has the cylinder missing and the hammer of the other has been snapped off), and one M16A2 (which is in excellent condition), two boxes of 5.56 ammunition (approximately one-hundred rounds each), three magazines of nine millimeter pistol ammunition, ten rounds of .22 ammunition, thirteen M.R.E.s, approximately twelve ACUs (riddled with bullet holes and drenched in blood), six BDUs (riddled with bullet holes and drenched in blood), five canteens (there were eight but three were full of holes), ten pairs of boots (none fit

Sukata nor myself), approximately forty meters of parachute

cord, approximately twenty-five meters of towing rope, three

chains (approximately four meters each), three forty liter jugs

of fuel, and three plate carriers (without plates).

I feel that we have a lot more useless items then we do

useful. Sukata felt somewhat the same but said that we may

be able to use the items for other purposes. I did not

understand what he was talking about but, I assume he will

figure something out.

I found that I do not hate Sukata as much as I had. I assume

that he had redeemed himself (somewhat) when he cleared

the house and allowed me to rest. I do not know how long

this time of peace will last but, I do believe I will try to make

amends with Sukata. I will wait until another day for that, for

we have much to do.

We have snuffed the fire outside and boarded up most every

opening in the house. We can only hope that the creatures are

not able to get in (in case we do return). I believe that my leg is beginning to feel better; my feet have dried and are not nearly as raw as they were yesterday, my broken ankle is no longer swollen, and my foot is no longer infected.

It is nearly time for us to leave and I must pack my bag and put my boots on. We may not survive this scouting mission so for those who find this: Do not let your guard down and never travel alone. I will continue my logs, if I live, as soon as I can.

Log Entry 35

I am nearly out of paper. If I do not find paper soon, I will not be able to continue my logs. I have approximately thirty-one pages left. If I must, I will resort to writing on the cover. I will search for a new notebook as soon as I have the chance. We have stopped to search a small gun shop. The shop is located near a small residential area. The signs indicate that it is reserved for military housing; thus, Sukata and I have come to the conclusion that we are near the base. We do not intend on returning to the small house from which we departed. Instead, we hope to find and secure a location much closer.

Sukata believes that we will not reach the base by first light, for there is still much distance between us and the base. Sukata suspects that we will not arrive at the base until nearly midday. I do not know exactly how far we are but, I am assuming Sukata is correct.

Once we are finished searching, we are to begin traveling again. The shop did not have any firearms or ammunition.

However, there may still be something of use. Since we opted to bring only what was needed, any extra equipment may prove to be essential.

Sukata and I decided to bring an M4 Carbine, all of the ammunition that we found, the five canteens, two of the nine millimeter pistols, the three plate carriers (without plates), the M.R.E.s, the cordage, an AR15, one of the chains, and approximately four liters of fuel (we had emptied some of the water bottles into the canteens).

I will continue my logs as soon as possible; for now I must help Sukata search.

Log Entry 36

I was not able to write last night because I lost my notebook while helping Sukata search.

We have left the small shop behind. Before we left, we took a final inventory of our equipment because Sukata said that we may not be able to find more supplies. After everything was tallied, we have: one AR15, one M4 Carbine, one .22 rifle, one .50 rifle, two nine millimeter pistols, one small .308 pistol, three plate carriers (without plates), approximately four liters of fuel, one-hundred-eighty-nine rounds of 5.56 mm ammunition, approximately four rounds of .308 ammunition, approximately thirty-one rounds of .50 ammunition, approximately thirty-two rounds of .22 ammunition, approximately forty meters of parachute cord, approximately twenty-five meters of tow rope, five one-liter canteens of water, one modified rat trap, one modified shotgun shell, twelve M.R.E.s, four four-liter jugs of water, three one-liter bottles of water, one chain (approximately four meters long), one glass shank, our survival knives, our two backpacks, our clothes, my pen, and my notebook. I have no idea what happened to the rest of our equipment. My only conclusion is that we must have left it behind when we hurried out of the mall.

Sukata wrapped the chain around his right arm and used a piece of wire he had found in the small shop to secure it. He said that it was a form of armor, making it easier to deal with the creatures. Once he was finished we began walking toward the military base again. Sukata estimated it two be approximately seven kilometers from our current location and said, "It may do us good to stop and scout every-so-often along the way." I understood why he suggested such after a mere fifteen minutes into our trip.

Sukata took its head off with such force that I thought he had broken his arm. It was absolutely amazing...Sukata reflexed when one of those creatures jumped from a bush alongside the road. His right arm swung, so fast that I nearly missed it, striking the creature across the face; imploding its head; causing teeth, blood, and brains to spray as though a small grenade had exploded inside the creature's skull. I stood there in awe while Sukata commenced to stomping the remainder of the creature's head until it was nothing more than a puddle of blood and pulp.

At that moment, I was torn. I did not know whether to continue hating Sukata or appreciate his company. I still have yet to come to a conclusion. I still want him to become badly injured but, I no longer want him to die. I believe that this may change; whether for bad or good.

We walked until it was about midday before Sukata decided that we needed to start scouting. Finding a small field, we stopped and rested while Sukata scoped the area with his .50 rifle. I sat quietly, awaiting his report.

Once he finished scouting, he turned to me and said, "The base isn't but a kilometer or so." Confused, I asked, "What do you mean? Surely it's farther than that." He stared at me and said, "I mean we are no more than a kilometer and a half away from the damn thing." I could not believe that we had made it; after all we had been through, we were finally within reach.

We waited around for a little while longer, scouted once more, and began to travel again. Sukata estimated that we should arrive at the base no later than dusk. I was becoming excited the closer we came. Sukata felt that I was getting my hopes up and told me to keep calm and alert.

We stopped approximately two-hundred meters from the gate of the base and scouted once more. Sukata reported, after a long period of scoping, that there was no movement anywhere in his field of view. I became overwhelmingly excited and blurted, "See? You were wrong. It's 'not' a death camp." He quickly responded with, "'Never' judge a book by its cover."

I stared at him in confusion for a few short moments before he explained, "Just because the cover looks good, does 'not' mean the story on the inside is." His analogy made much more sense once he explained it to me. I had heard the same analogy several times before this all happened but only used when explaining people, never a place. Despite my reluctance to believe Sukata, I knew that he was correct; even though the outside areas looked clear, the inside could be teeming with those creatures.

Sukata decided that we would use the guard tower near the gate for shelter until we felt well enough to begin scouting. He explained that we should explore the base a little at a time, clearing each area before we continue, until we find the building containing the desired artifacts. I agreed and opted to follow his plan.

The skies began to darken before we managed to get inside the guard tower. The door had a superior locking mechanism that caused many issues for Sukata. When he finally managed to break the door handle off, he shoved the muzzle of the .308 pistol into the hole and stepped to one side. I was confused by his action until he asked, "You just gonna stand there and try to catch the ricochet or are you going to get the hell out of the way?" I realized what he intended to do and moved out of the way.

The shot rang out, loudly. When Sukata removed the pistol,

the other door handle had been blown into the small corridor in the other side. He squatted down and looked inside. I stood to his right, watching him. He lifted the pistol up to the hole again, aimed and fired two more shots with a short pause in between. I continued to watch him as he aimed and fired once more. When he finished, he used the tip of his survival knife to pry the bolt loose from the inside of the door.

When he finished all of that, the door still would not open. Sukata stared at it for a moment and then came to the conclusion that there was another "force" working against him (his words). I did not understand until he ripped a panel from the outside wall, using his survival knife, ripped some wire free and then kicked the door in.

Once we were inside, we searched to ensure nothing else was in the building with us. Sukata went back to the door, closed it, and used the chain to secure it to the railing that was bolted to the concrete wall that enclosed the stairwell. He then continued to search the edge of the door as though he were looking for something significant.

When Sukata returned, he did not explain himself and I did not question his logic. Instead, we sat down and enjoyed the cool evening for a few moments.

After those few moments of peaceful silence, I began to talk to Sukata in hopes of making amends to a short extent and to pass the time. I began the conversation with a few questions: "What's the plan?" "What are we going to look for?" "How long do you think we will be here?" He replied with his usual smartass remarks and comical lines by which he did not intend to offend me but, come extremely close to doing so. Sukata and I spoke for some time while I wrote my log. I am exhausted and sore. I am going to attempt to sleep while it is still peaceful. I will continue my logs as soon as possible, for we are to scout the first block of the military base tomorrow which may take a while.

In case I die before my next log: If you have read this, I hope that you do not make the same mistakes as I did and I wish you the best. And remember: "Don't over think things, just shut up and do what needs to be done to survive." ~Sukata

Log Entry 37

I awoke to find Sukata missing. I have no idea where he went or how he got out. The door was still chained shut and the windows are still intact. He is not on the balcony that wraps around the top of the tower either. I have yet to find any way of opening the windows or any form of hatch through which he could have exited.

I have waited for several hours and have searched every centimeter of this tower. Sukata's gear is here; along with mine. His machete is gone but nothing else has been taken. I am unsure of his reasoning for leaving. I have, however, discovered that I am beginning to feel hatred for him, again. It is not the same hatred as before. This hatred is more similar to the hatred one might have if someone were to leave them behind during a game or vacation. The hatred is directed more toward his actions rather than him.

It has been hours since I awoke and still no sign of Sukata. Searching the tower has arisen more questions than it answered. I have decided that I will wait until morning before I leave in search of him. If he has not returned by then, I can only assume he is either dead or trapped somewhere. Despite these possibilities, I still intend to search for him, for, if nothing else, peace at mind.

I fear that he may have left me to my own devices but why would he leave his equipment? The circumstances of which he has left are a mystery to me. I do not understand why he would leave his equipment if he intended to leave me. This leaves only one plausible explanation: he plans to return. But why would he only take his machete and not water or food in case something happened?

Scouting, using Sukata's rifle, has yet to produce any sign of any creatures. In fact, I have yet to see any movement. It is eerily still outside, as though time itself has stopped. There is no wind, no animals roaming, no birds chirping; I have yet to see even, so much as, a fly. I have a feeling similar to that that someone may have when awaiting their death.

I have grown sick of sitting here, waiting for something to happen. The silence is beginning to get to me and I have nothing to keep my mind off of it. I have attempted several times to distract myself, to no avail. The longer I sit here, the more I think about the situation I am in. Thinking of such things causes me much heart ache. I will not write of this for it is of no importance.

It is near night and I have yet to see any signs of Sukata. I even went outside earlier in hope of finding some clues but found nothing. I searched the outside of the tower, finding nothing. I walked to the gate and searched the other side as best I could; nothing. I cannot, for the life of me, think of anything that would explain Sukata's disappearance. It is as though he vanished into thin air.

I shall continue to search for him from the safety of the tower. I can only hope that he will appear on the other side of the fence or somewhere in the surrounding fields. I may not be able to see him due to the lack of light but, I am still going to put forth an effort. The least I could do, for all that he has done for me, is keep trying.

It is midnight and I have heard a tapping noise expelling

from the door for some time now. I was confused at first by the noise, trying to find the source but, soon discovered it was coming from the door. I did not approach the door due to the fear of the noise being produced by one of those creatures. I have tried to see the outside of the door from the inside but, have been unsuccessful in finding a location from which the door can be viewed. I finally resorted to keeping quiet and writing in hope that it will stop soon.

It is nearly daylight now. The noise has persisted; at one point I had to stop writing because it became louder. I do not know what it is but I am too fearful to open the door. I have attempted several times to conceive another method which would allow me to see the source of the sound, but I have failed. If the sound continues, I will open the door despite my fears.

Log Entry 38

Sukata has returned. I found myself feeling relieved when I saw him walking across the field. He explained everything to me as I sat and listened. I did not understand much of it not because of Sukata's explanation, but because I do not recall such events. I will start from where I left off the night before last.

The tapping noise stopped late in the morning. I became worried that whatever it was that was making the noise had found a way in. I grabbed a nine millimeter pistol, checked to make sure it was loaded, and then walked down to the door. I waited there, silently, for some time before I decided that it was clear to open the door.

Upon opening the door, I saw Sukata walking, beaten and worn, through the field across the road from the tower. Relieved and excited, I began to walk toward him. I made it nearly across the road when he looked up, noticed me, and began to yell something that I could not make out. I became extremely curious as Sukata began to run toward me, waving his machete, and yelling. I simply kept walking, smiling. I did not know that he was trying to warn me about the group of creatures that was coming toward me.

I heard the coughing noises when it was too late. I was already across the road and too far from the tower to make it back. I did not know what to do. Sukata began waving his machete, giving me instructions to run for the gate. I hesitated, but then followed his orders. I only had thirteen shots in the pistol. I would not have been able to kill but one or two of the creatures and there had to have been at least a dozen.

I ran for the gate as fast as I could; having to use crutches made this very difficult and I could not move very fast because of it. As I neared the gate, Sukata was nearing me. I still could not hear him very well; the creatures made it even harder for me to make out what he was yelling. It took a moment to understand what he was trying to tell me but, I, eventually, understood and began to climb the gate as fast as I could, leaving my crutches behind.

Sukata began climbing the fence, near his location, as I neared the top of the gate. When I reached the top, I did not know how to get down. Too afraid to jump, for fear of damaging my leg further, I held on to the top of the gate and awaited instruction from Sukata.

The creatures reached the gate, increasing my anxiety and causing me to falter. It felt like an eternity had passed before I heard Sukata's voice again. He kept yelling, "Jump! Jump! Jump!" but I could not move. I was too scared to let go of the gate.

Sukata was nearly to the gate when he yelled, "You either jump or I'm leaving you there!" With the words 'leaving you there' sinking deep into my mind, I concluded that I was either going to die trying to get away or die of starvation. Because the second option would be more painful than Sukata killing me if I were bitten, I gathered my courage and jumped as far away from the gate as I could.

Landing hard on the ground, I heard my right leg make a loud snapping noise and intense sensations of pain began to shoot up my leg. Sukata ran to me, grabbed my arm and began dragging me. By this time, my adrenaline was flowing and the pain began to subside and I passed out.

I awoke in a small, dark room. Sukata was standing on the opposing side of the room looking through a small gap between the door and the door frame. I was still quite groggy and could not think very clearly. I could not see very well, for my vision was quite blurred. I could not speak because I could not think clearly enough to do so.

With the pain in my leg growing to an unbearable intensity, my stomach became upset, my mind became foggier, and my vision became worse due to tears. I felt nearly helpless; unable to beg for death and unable to do it myself, I began to beat my head against the wall.

Sukata became curious of my actions and approached me. Startled when I felt him touch my arm, I jerked, twisting my leg, causing even more pain. I passed out, again.

When I awoke, again, I was still unable to think and see clearly. I could focus enough to tell that we were outside but nothing more. I, still, could not speak. I turned my head in hope of seeing Sukata nearby, but could not make anything out.

I assume Sukata understood and began to speak. I could make out most of what he said but, not all of it, "Don't trip...I don't think we can...our stuff, those cre...I might try to get in...but I don't know if I can...you might die...back. I need to get you ins...somewhere befo...I...you get bitten...kill you...don't worry..." I failed to hear the rest as I began to pass out again.

When I awoke for the third time, I was not nearly as groggy and could think somewhat clearly. Sukata had dragged me into another dark building. He was standing at the door, peering through the gap between it and the door frame. I asked, "Where...we?" He understood despite the slur and replied, "In a small storage shed. We aren't but thirty meters from the gate. Those zombies are gone but, I don't know where they went and I don't want to leave you alone in case they show up again."

I sat there quietly, awaiting Sukata's next move, fighting the pain in my leg. I asked Sukata what happened to him explaining that I had no memory of him leaving. He shut the door and sat down in front of it (assuming by the distant sound of his voice) and said "You've got to be going crazy or something." He began to tell me about the day he disappeared.

He explained how he had spotted the woman that shot him, grabbed his machete, and ran after her, having me close the door behind him. He went on to tell me about tracking the woman through the fields and into the forest. He paused for a while getting up to watch out the door.

When he closed the door again, it was night. He sat down again or at least leaned against the door and began to tell his tale again, "I tracked her until she disappeared on me. It was getting dark and I could hardly see where I was going." He paused for a second (I assume listening) and then continued, "I know she isn't that damn sneaky so, I don't know what the hell happened to her. I guess I just fell too far behind to watch which way she went. It's not hard to lose someone in the woods." He stopped again, this time shifting around to peek out the door.

He continued, "When I couldn't figure out where she went, I stopped and listened for a while, then headed back." I became restless as my leg began to throb harder, causing me to try and pull myself up to a more comfortable sitting position. Once I found a spot that felt better, I began to listen again. "…That's when I looked up and saw you and that small horde."

Finishing his story, he stood again and began watching through the gap in the door again. I sat there quietly, waiting for an update. Sukata said, "Alright, here's the plan: I'm going to drag you over to the door here, make a run for it and you keep the door shut until I get back." As he spoke, he walked to me and grabbed my arm. Intense pain shot through my leg as he dragged me to the door but, I knew that it had to be done.

Sukata dragged me until I was against the door, and then

opened it while I leaned forward, and made a run for it. I leaned hard against the door and awaited his return.

When he came back, he had most of our equipment and told me that the group the creatures found a hole in the fence or there are more of them. He did not hesitate nor did he warn me as he grabbed my arm and began dragging me toward another building.

Once inside the new building, he left me be, built a small fire and told me to get some rest. I explained that I could not sleep due to the pain of my leg. He understood and took watch.

I am near passing out again so I will end it here for now. I will continue my logs, if possible, as soon as possible; for now I am going to rest.

Log Entry 39

When I awoke, Sukata was dragging me, once again, to another building. I could feel my leg contorting with every centimeter we traveled, sending intense pains up my leg, causing me to grunt in agony. Sukata must have heard me because he hushed me and whispered, "They're close…trying to get somewhere safer…"

I controlled the grunting as best I could as Sukata continued to drag me between the vehicles scattered about the parking lot. I could not tell which part of the base we were at, but I could see the Commissary at the end of the parking lot, approximately forty meters away from where we were. I was curious as to why we were traveling away from the source of food; until I saw the creatures.

The entire window in the front of the building was covered in bloody smears as the creatures inside clawed and chewed at the glass. I could nearly see their faces but, there was too much blood to make them out.

I could not see where Sukata was taking me, but I knew that

it was not the PX, for the PX was across the parking lot to my right. I assumed at that moment that Sukata was trying to get to the armory or the barracks; but, I was unsure.

We were nearly to Sukata's chosen location when he began to accelerate. I did not understand why he began hurrying. He did not say anything and I was afraid to speak for fear of alerting any creatures nearby. I wanted to scream because Sukata's speed caused my leg to falter to and fro. The pain became so intense that I passed out, again.

When I awoke, again, I found myself in a large building. Sukata was curiously staring out of a window; which was approximately three meters from me. I stared at him for a while and then asked, "Where are we?" Without hesitation and without looking at me, he simply replied, "Don't know." Confused, I sat quietly for a long moment and then asked, "What's the plan then?" Again, without looking at me and without hesitation, he replied, "Don't know."

Since I was getting nowhere, asking questions, I sat there quietly for some time. I tried to figure out a way to get answers, but could not think of any way to do so without having to ask Sukata. Instead, I decided that I would try to decipher the puzzle by myself.

Upon examination from my position, it seems that we are in a garage of some sort. There are several vehicles parked in a strange array with nearly every hood propped open and the doors left open as though people had gotten out of them in haste. I could not see much more than that for the lighting was too poor.

Sukata, eventually, left his position at the window and walked over to me. I watched him closely as though he were going to do something to me. When he sat down next to me, I felt relieved that he was not going to begin dragging me again or try to set my leg.

He looked at me and asked, "How's the leg?" I wanted to yell, 'How do you think it is?!' but I knew he meant well so I, instead, said, "It feels like someone crushed it with a sledge hammer or something." He said, "I figured, considering it's completely shattered." I sat there, thinking, for a moment and then asked, "How do you know it's shattered?" "I tried to set it for you, while you were out," he replied. I appreciated his consideration.

We sat there for some time before Sukata decided that we should eat. While he was preparing an M.R.E., I asked him, "Why were you looking outside and what happened to those creatures?" He didn't look at me but, explained that he was watching the horde that has formed outside and that the creatures he referred to earlier were probably among them. I was shocked by the update and insisted that Sukata explain to me how we ended up in this situation. He began to tell me everything, trying to supply as much detail as possible, most likely to pass the time.

He told me that soon after I went to sleep, a few creatures began to appear from different areas of the base. Continuing, he explained that he decided that our location would have been over taken had we not moved and began dragging me toward another small building. He said that when we arrived at the entrance of the building, he could hear creatures inside, "stirring 'round" and decided that it would not be a good idea to try to clear them out. He paused for a few moments while he concentrated on what he was doing. I noticed that he was shaking badly and I asked, "What's wrong?"

He did not answer and continued with his story, explaining how he had dragged me into a garage, here on the base, and that there was oil and blood covering the ground so he had to pick me up and throw me over his shoulder, and how he was amazed that I did not awaken. He said that once we made it through the garage, he laid me on the ground again, tried to set my leg and began to drag me once more. By this time, in his story, it was nearly daylight and I was still "out cold." Again, he paused for a moment as he cleaned up the mess he had made, gathered the food, and returned to me.

I sat quietly, eating, waiting for him to continue. He spoke between bites of food but, only after swallowing what food he had in his mouth. He began again where he had left off, telling me about how he had dragged me to the Commissary in hope of there being few people there when the "outbreak" occurred but, to his amazement there were dozens of creatures inside. He took a bite of food, chewed, and swallowed.

"I wasn't gonna try the PX so I just kept dragging you," he continued, "then I saw all those zombies coming our way and sped up, trying to get here before they caught up with us." I sat in silence while I thought about everything he had said, trying to put the pieces that I was missing together.

When we finished eating, it was around midday. Sukata got up and began exploring the vehicles that lay scattered about the building. I could not move so, I sat there, and contemplated our situation. Every few moments, Sukata would give me an update of his findings.

Once he had finished his search, he returned and explained that there was nothing of use in any of them. He then said, "Before night arrives, we need to get somewhere better than this." I agreed, but did not know how we were going to get out of the building we were in. We had most of our gear but there were too many creatures to try and kill; besides, shooting them would have attracted more to our location. Sukata wandered the building for some time, trying to put together a plan. I sat where I was, trying not to make too much noise. I wished that I could have helped Sukata but was unable to.

When Sukata noticed that I felt helpless and unneeded, he handed me the gear and told me to do an inventory, load all of the firearms, and try to find something that would help us out of this situation. I did as he asked.

Altogether, we had an AR15, approximately one-hundred-twenty rounds of 5.56 mm ammunition, one nine millimeter pistol (I must have dropped the other one when I jumped), twenty-two rounds of 9 mm ammunition, one .50 rifle, approximately twenty-eight round of .50 ammunition, four canteens of water, one four-liter jug of water, eight M.R.E.s, approximately six rounds of .22 ammunition, approximately forty meters of parachute cord, a broken rat trap, one one-liter bottle of fuel, two plate carriers (which we are wearing), a chain approximately four meters in length (which is still wrapped around Sukata's arm), our survival knives, our two backpacks, our clothes, my pen, and my notebook.

I set the one-liter bottle of fuel aside with the reasoning that Sukata could use it as a Molotov, provided he found a glass bottle, which could be used to distract the creatures long enough for us to escape. I then, packed everything neatly into one bag. Since I am unable to carry one of them, there is no need for Sukata to struggle with both of them.

When he finished roaming around, he sat down next to me and asked, "So what's the verdict?" I explained about the bag and the Molotov. He thought the Molotov might be our only option and began searching for a glass container of some sort.

While he was searching, I began writing. It was dusk before Sukata came back with a large glass jar which was missing the lid. He explained that we had to find something to "plug it up" but, we would have to wait until morning because it is too dark to see. I agreed with him and he went back to his position at the window.

I am tired and in an immense amount of pain. I will continue writing as soon as possible. In case I do not make it through the night: I hope that you have better luck than we did.

Log Entry 40

My plan was successful…somewhat.

Sukata was awake before first light, searching the building again for something to use as a lid for the jar he had found last night. I awoke to the noise of him rummaging through some broken crates. Worried that the noise was being produce by the creatures, I jerked, twisting my leg, forcing me to scream in pain.

Sukata immediately stopped what he was doing and ran to see what the problem was. After I explained what had happened, he told me that I need to chill out and quit being so jumpy. As he walked away, he said, "It's okay to be a little paranoid, but jumpiness will get you, as you just found out, hurt or even killed."

It seemed like hours had passed before Sukata announced that he had found something that would work. Excitedly, he ran back to me and grabbed the jar. Testing the object, which seemed to be a fuel tank cap, he found that it was slightly too small. Disappointed, but not discouraged, Sukata ran toward one of the vehicles, reached into the engine compartment and removed something. He removed his knife from its sheath and began carving on whichever component he had removed from the engine.

Only moments had passed, before Sukata returned with the jar, a piece of rubber, and the lid. He retrieved the bottle of fuel and poured approximately half of it into the jar. Once he had the amount that he wanted in the jar, he ripped a strip of cloth from the lower portion of his shirt, stuffed it into the jar and then pulled it out, partially, and then used the rubber and the cap to hold the cloth in place.

When he finished rigging his device together, he walked toward the window, set the Molotov on the ground, walked around for a moment, and then picked something up from the floorboard of one of the vehicles. He then returned to the jar, set a piece of paper or something similar on the ground and returned to me. "How are we gonna light it?" he asked me. I did not know how to answer him, we had been using the heat packs found in the M.R.E.s to cook with and they would not produce enough heat to start a fire. Sukata began pacing, thinking of a way he could start a fire. It did not take long as he ran to one of the vehicles, climbed in, and reached under the dash.

He arose from the vehicle holding a long piece of wire, ran to the jar, grabbed the paper, and ran back to the vehicle.

Confused, I sat there and watched him as he connected one end of the wire to something and then held the paper close to the other while he stroked it against something else which created sparks.

It took some time before Sukata managed to get the paper to burn. As soon as a flame appeared, Sukata walked, carefully, toward the jar again, holding the paper as though it were a heart and he a surgeon. With great concentration, he lowered the flame to the cloth hanging from the jar and let it catch flame; quickly, he waved the paper to put it out and grabbed the jar.

Opening a window, Sukata took aim, focused, and then hurled the jar as far as he could. When it hit, he became excited and said, "Got it." I sat there, smiling, awaiting his update.

Sukata had landed the jar on a vehicle. The fire that resulted was slow but effective at keeping the creatures distracted. Sukata seemed to enjoy the show as he watched the vehicle burn as though he were a young child watching fireflies at night.

Once Sukata was satisfied with the creatures' distraction, we moved while we had the chance. Sukata began dragging me once more, this time by the arm rather than my plate carrier (the drag strap was beginning to tear). We headed toward a nearby building that had no markings but, was quite fortified. Sukata assumed it was either an armory or brig.

When we arrived, Sukata used his knocking technique. He did not like what he heard, but he said that there must not be too many because they are not making a lot of noise. He hesitated and then decided to go in despite the creatures on the inside.

Sukata let go of my arm, leaving me to lie on the ground.

Opening the door, he was nearly knocked down by one of the creatures inside. Sukata reacted quickly and shoved his chain-wrapped arm into the creature's mouth. I could only see part of the action, upside-down, by tilting my head backwards.

With the arm in the creature's mouth, Sukata jerked, twisting the creature's neck, causing it to make a loud snapping noise; I knew, then, that he had broken the creature's neck. Sukata must have overexerted himself because he sat there for a moment before kicking the creature in the head and then standing up. He stood there for a moment, catching his breath and then returned to retrieve me.

Grabbing my arm, he said, "Bastards are getting tougher or I'm getting weaker...let's hope for the latter." I understood that he was joking but it was no time for laughter; we had to get somewhere safe and quick.

Once we were inside, Sukata closed the door and checked the other doors in the room. All were securely locked. Sukata explained that he was too tired to fight anymore and that we would, instead, hold out here for the night. When first light comes, he expects to begin exploring the rest of the building.

We know there are creatures behind each of the other three doors in the room because we can hear them scratching and biting at the doors. Sukata guesses that there is one behind the door farthest to the left, three behind the middle door, and he cannot tell how many behind the third.

For now, I believe that we will regain our strength in hope of making progress tomorrow.

Log Entry 41

Before the first sign of light, I was awakened by a horrid sound coming from behind the door farthest to the left. It sounded as though one of the creatures had caught fire, was trapped, or something and began to screech in pain.

When I looked around, Sukata was still asleep. I found this unusual, but did not question it, for he had over exerted himself several times to get us thus far. I, instead, awaited a change in the creature's tone, hoping that it would die.

Hours had passed, it seemed, and the creature was still screeching. I kept an eye on the door in case the creature decided to attempt to break it down. Every few moments, I would glance at Sukata who was sitting against the wall to my right, holding his machete in his right hand, still sleeping. I began to presume him dead but, was not able to check; nor was I able to see him breathing; Sukata breathes quite shallow when he sleeps.

Despite the constant screeching from the creature, the other creatures behind the center-most door could be audibly heard. They seemed to increase in their activity as the screeching continued. I became worried that they would soon be able to get through the door and began to try to awaken Sukata.

It only took one time of whispering Sukata's name for him to awaken; it seemed as though he was not asleep and instead resting his eyes. Once I knew he was awake and focused, I directed him to the doors.

At first, he seemed to be confused and then he arose and carefully walked to the door from which the screeching was radiating. When he reached the door, he set his ear to the steel and listened. He made a few strange expressions and then stepped away from the door.

The screeching continuing, he began to pace again; as though he were thinking or concentrating on how to handle the situation. Hours seemed to pass before he approached the door again. This time, he grabbed the handle as though he were going to try to open the door; it seemed as though Sukata wanted to tear the door from its hinges.

After a few moments, Sukata stepped away from the door again. Without saying anything, he walked to his bag, opened it, and pulled out the parachute cord. Confused and intrigued, I watched him as he approached the door again, tying a lasso with the parachute cord.

When he reached the door, he slid the parachute cord through the gap at the floor and wriggled it. I watched in curiosity as he "fished" for the creature. I felt as though I were a child watching his father attempt to coax an animal out of hiding. It was not long before something happened, as Sukata had planned; because he had pulled the cord taut and held it in place. Watching him seemed like watching a fisherman reeling in a large fish with his bare hands.

Sukata held kept the line taut as he tried to find something to tie it to. I realized what he was doing and began searching the room, with my eyes, in hope of helping him, as best I could. I searched vigorously and then spotted a steel plate bolted to the floor that acted as a door stop. I quickly pointed it out to him and he appreciatively accepted the idea, tying the parachute cord around it.

Once he had the cord tied off, he returned to his equipment, grabbed his .50 rifle and then returned to the door. He stood there for a moment, speaking under his breath as though he were speaking to his rifle, and then began to hammer at the door handle using the butt-plate of the rifle.

It took quite a few strikes before the door handle came free. Sukata quickly ripped the remainder of the handle from the door and shoved the interior components through the other side. It seemed that he was becoming increasingly angry, as the creature continued to screech.

Sukata peeked through the hole in the door and then returned to his equipment, set his rifle down, grabbed the nine millimeter pistol, and then returned to the door. As he approached the door, he slid the muzzle of the pistol into the hole, pressed himself against the wall, forcing the pistol to an awkward angle, paused, took a deep breath, and fired.

With that single shot, the screeching ended. Sukata seemed to be relieved and lowered the pistol to his side. He stood there for a moment and then set his back against the wall, lowered his head, and slid down to the floor. I waited for a few moments before I began to speak to him.

"You alright?" I asked. Sukata did not raise his head but replied, "Yeah, just annoyed by that damn thing." I sat there quietly for a moment and then began to question him as to what the plan was. He explained that he was going to open the door, stomp the creature's head until it was mush for annoying him, and then continue on, exploring what is "behind door number one."

I felt the plan was suitable and requested that he leave me armed in case something went wrong while he was gone. He agreed, walked over to me and handed me the nine millimeter pistol and the remaining rounds, saying, "Don't lose this one," with a grin of serious humor on his face. He then walked to his gear again, grabbed the AR15 and a handful of rounds, stuck the rounds in his pocket, checked the chamber and the magazine, tapped the magazine against his boot, slapped it back into the rifle, and then walked to the door once more.

Sukata used his knife to pry the bolt from the door as he had at the tower. Once he had the door open, the scene became a frenzy of blood-splattering stomps, causing loud crunching and squishing noises to emanate from the creature's skull. The sounds sickened me, nearly causing me to vomit. I forced myself to ignore the sounds and concentrated on something else, fearing dehydration would only accelerate, had I vomited.

When Sukata was finished (several moments later), he let out a sigh of satisfaction and continued on into the new frontier. He quickly disappeared behind the door as he rounded a corner using the technique most militant units use (I believe he referred to it as "cutting the pie").

It seemed eternity had passed before Sukata returned. As he walked out of the door, he had a grin on his face. I was surprised by this as I rarely saw such. He seemed to be quite happy considering the situation we were in.

When he reached me, he asked, "How would you like a steak

dinner?" I smiled as large as I could and said, "I would 'love' a steak dinner." With a sinister grin, he said, "Well I'm sorry, we're fresh out of that but we do have…" He removed a bag of beef jerky from under his shirt. I became excited at the idea of having some form of meat other than the "mystery meat" found in the M.R.E.s.

Sukata sat down next to me and explained that there was nothing but offices behind "door number one" so there was no need to really search there unless we think something may be of use. He handed me a piece of beef jerky and told me to make it last because we were going to ration it out.

We sat there for a while enjoying our piece of beef jerky and talked about how he planned to handle the three creatures behind "door number two." When we finished eating, Sukata retrieved the parachute cord, being careful not to get blood on him, and then repeated the same experiment with the creatures behind the second door.

Within moments, he had captured one of the creatures and tied the cord to the door stop again. He said he did not know exactly how he was going to pull this one off without something going wrong but, he was going to try anyway. "Shoot me if I get bitten," were his words to me as he retrieved his .50 rifle again.

He repeated the same procedure, beating the handle off the door, grabbing the pistol, and shooting the creature he had tied down. He then untied the cord, tied a lasso in the other end and began "fishing for a second creature. Once he had one captured, he pulled the cord taut and wrapped it around the door stop. He inserted the muzzle of the pistol into the hole and shot the second creature. Upon completion of the second one, he began to think again.

Moments passed, and then Sukata cut the parachute cord as close to the door as he could and tied another lasso. He attempted, once more, to "fish" for the third creature but failed to capture it as he did the others. Becoming aggravated, he pried the bolt free from the door, while leaning against the door, and slowly opened it until the creature stuck its arm through.

Laughing at the creature, Sukata grabbed its arm and shoved it against the wall, snapping it. Surprised by his actions, I cringed and began to wonder who he had become. I did not react to the act of violence and, instead, turned away. I heard two shots and assumed that he had shot the creature.

Knowing that he intended to stomp the creatures' heads, I did not turn and instead closed my eyes.

Sukata approached me and asked, "What's wrong?" I did not reply. He said, "Oh, you think I'm going crazy. Don't you? Well, I remember someone who peeled the back of his fucking skull off and didn't remember a damn thing of it. I'm not crazy, I'm just not weak and I live for this shit." I thought about what he said and then asked a series of questions that I did not believe I would get answers for.

As expected, Sukata answered the questions with as vague an answer as possible or answered in such a way that it could be perceived in several different manners. I gave up and decide that some things were best left alone. I knew that Sukata had lived a different life than most, but I could not get him to say much about it. He would give me bland bits of his story but never any details.

Sukata decided that we would sleep in the offices, because we could easily barricade ourselves in, if need be. Agreeing, but regretting having to be moved, I lifted my right leg and laid it atop my left leg. This caused me a significant amount of pain, causing me to nearly pass out. Sukata did not wait for my leg to quit hurting and began to drag me while he explained, "'I'd' rather deal with it all at once than have to deal with it twice."

It is nearly midnight and Sukata intends to move me, again, tomorrow so I must rest. I will continue my logs as soon as possible. If I am not able to continue my logs, remember this: No matter where you go, 'no' place is safe, some may be 'safer' but 'none' are safe.

Log Entry 42

I slept through the day, yesterday; Sukata seemed to have done the same. Sukata awoke me late in the night, telling me that we had wasted an entire day. I could not believe it. He did not waste any more time and began searching for something.

I noticed, while watching Sukata, that I was experiencing a strange sensation of overwhelming exhaustion as though my body were lacking oxygen. It felt as though my body was trying to go to "sleep" or become numb. I did not understand the sensation. I, soon, realized that I could not think clearly either; my thoughts became disseminated and my vision became distorted. I began to worry that I had contracted something.

Sukata wandered around for quite a while, disappearing in the corridor through which we came. I did not know what he was looking for; nor did I have any idea of what he had planned or realized, but I was certain it was important.

It felt as though another eternity had passed when I heard

Sukata say something to himself; cussing. His voice was followed by a series of creaks and squeals; as though metal were being bent or two pieces were scraping one another. I did not understand the source of the sounds until Sukata returned.

Sukata did not hesitate. He quickly grabbed me by the arm and began dragging me toward the corridor. I could not think clearly enough to question his reasoning but, I assumed that he knew what he was doing.

Once we reached the end of the corridor, Sukata pulled the door open and dragged me into the lobby, once more. In seconds Sukata had dragged me across the room near the main entrance and returned to the door, closing it securely. I still did not understand why he did such; but knew that there had to be some intelligent thought behind his actions.

Breaking several windows, using the barrel of his .50 rifle, Sukata seemed to relax slightly. He seemed as though he had found the source of our suffering and was exiling it from existence. I sat quietly as I awaited an explanation. Sukata returned to me with a confused and yet angry expression upon his face. I did not understand why; but I felt I would soon.

His voice full of anger; not directed toward me, seemingly more toward himself; he began to explain that when he shot the first creature, the round must have penetrated the opposing side of his skull and damaged one of the gas line that were behind the sheet rock covering the wall. I remained quiet as I attempted to regain my composure.

Still unable to think clearly, I tried to ask Sukata a question, "Why we feel this way?" He understood and answered, "You feel the way you do, because you have inhaled a lot of gas, whereas I myself inhaled just as much as you, my body is more immune to such things and, also, is not trying to compensate for an injury. Thus, your immune system is quite low, mine is not. Don't get me wrong I feel sick and have a headache but, no worse than I did breathing the fumes from the acids and various other chemicals I used to work with."

What Sukata said made sense but, it did not set my mind at

ease. I attempted to ask another question, "Permanent?" He looked at me. "It can be. I don't know, it just depends on how your body handles it." I began worry; even more than before. Sukata watched me for a while; checking, every few moments, to make sure I was recovering without any complications; as he, once more, began to conceive a plan to breach the final door.

He disappeared behind the second door several times, returning with pieces of desks and tables. I became confused by his actions.

My confusion was only increased when he emerged from the door holding a large set of keys with a grin on his face. I stared at him for a moment and then grinned, realizing the significance of his find.

I could hear the creatures become more active as Sukata collected the parachute cord from the bodies of the creatures that were behind "door number two." Sukata did not seem to worry and placed his machete on the ground next to him. The creatures' activity increased as Sukata began to break, chop, and tie several pieces of the broken desks and table together, forming a shield of sorts.

When he finished, he tested his "shield" out, ensuring that it was durable enough to withstand the abuse that the creatures would impose upon it; it seemed to satisfy Sukata. He lifted the device using his left arm, leaving his right, which had the chain wrapped around it, free. He retrieved the ring of keys, placing it on a screw or nail that was protruding from the shield. He, then, retrieved his machete and tapped it against the front of the shield as though he were a warrior preparing for battle.

Once Sukata was prepared, he approached the door and began to test key after key until he found one that allowed the lock to turn. Without hesitation, Sukata braced himself, turned the key and knob at the same time, and threw the door open.

To his surprise and mine, there were no creatures at its threshold as we had suspected. The creatures could be heard clearly as their coughs and growls echoed through the corridor on the opposing side of the door.

By this time, I had recovered most of my former self and asked, "What? Where are they?" Sukata did not answer and instead, slowly, entered the corridor, turning right and disappearing behind the wall. I awaited his return for an update, hoping that all would be well and that we had nothing to worry about.

When Sukata appeared from the corridor, he stared at me as though I were something of interest. I became leery of Sukata's thoughts. He approached me with a sinister expression and said, "I found the armoury…only issue is…I don't know where the ammo is. Also, though zombies we're hearing are down in the basement of this place. There's a cell door keeping them from gettin' to us but I can't say for certain what else is down there. We might have to open the door, which would let them loose, to see."

I did not want to think of those creatures being loose…with us…locked in a building…with 'no' way out. I assumed that Sukata would have a plan to deal with them so I agreed that we should open the door if he felt it was needed. He accepted my answer and quickly grabbed my arm and began dragging me toward the cell door.

Once we arrived in the room that contained the weapons' containment cell, Sukata dragged me to the wall across from the stairs to the basement. I could see the light beginning to shine through the window high above the floor as daylight peeked over the horizon.

Sukata handed me the nine millimeter pistol and walked toward the stairs across from me that led to the cell door. I heard the creatures' coughs and growls become louder as he approached them. I was not worried about Sukata but, I was worried 'for' Sukata. I knew that he could handle himself, but I did not know how things would play out.

It was nearly midday before Sukata climbed the stairs from the basement. I could not believe that he had taken so long to complete the task; as he usually made quick work of anything that hindered his progression.

When he returned, he was saddened because there was no

ammunition; that he could find, for any of the firearms. I, too, became saddened at his prospect, having hoped for even a subtle break of luck. It was, yet, another disappointment to add to the series of misfortunes that has plagued our journey from the start.

Sukata explained that he had cleared the basement and that he believes that it was used as a "safe room" of sorts. "Problem is the morons didn't realize that once you're bitten, there is no saving you," he commented. I agreed, but felt that Sukata was not giving them the proper recognition for not knowing what they were dealing with.

We did not talk much for the rest of the day and, instead, contemplated our next move as this one was a complete waste of time and resources. We did not settle on a target destination nor did we come to a conclusion as to how we were going to get out of here. We, finally, decided that it was of no use trying to map everything out as we did not know the circumstances in which we would be leaving this place. Sukata handed me another piece of beef jerky and said, "It's been a shitty day." He was correct and he knew it.

We sat there against the wall and enjoyed our beef jerky, nibble by nibble, as I wrote. It is nearly too dark to see now as it nears night, thus I shall leave my reader(s) with this: Never use a firearm in a closed area if you intend to stay there long; misfortunes may come of it.

Log Entry 43

He has me chained to the railing near the wall opposite of the stairwell entrance. I understand it is for his safety and agreed to it as long as he provided food and water. He has agreed to put me out of my misery once I have become a danger.

It was early morning when Sukata decided to drag me into the weapons' containment cell. He said that it would be safer, if we were able to close ourselves in, if the creatures somehow got into the building. I agreed with the idea; besides, that would give us a chance to repair our firearms if we could, and would allow for a "safe" place to sleep; considering there is only one way in and no existence of windows. I did not find out until it was too late, exactly how wrong I was.

Once Sukata dragged me into the room, he helped me find a comfortable spot and examined my leg. The bruising was severe and the swelling was finally descending. I was amazed at how badly it was damaged; considering I had not seen it since before the jump. I would never have guessed that it would be so horrid.

Sukata explained that there were only two options when dealing with a break so severe; without proper medical attention. He explained that we could, either, cast it and hope that it heals well enough to function or we could remove the leg at the knee, bandage it, and use a prosthetic of sorts, fashioned from things we find. I questioned him about his opinion, the odds of functionality, and the timeframes before I would be able to walk.

Sukata sat down in front of me with one of his legs bent and lying flat on the ground and the other bent with his foot flat on the ground. Using his knee as an arm rest, he looked at me as though I were a cancer patient. I stared back, awaiting his reply, in suspense.

In a calm and yet excited tone, he began, "If it were me I'd just hack the damn thing off. I know that sounds rough but it's your best option. If you cast it, you won't be able to use it for months and even then we don't know if it will heal right. On the other hand, if you cut it off, you could bleed out. If we keep you from bleeding out and bandage it up right, you would be able to walk on it within a day or two; it would just hurt like hell." He paused for a moment and then continued, "I myself would've hacked it off the first day…dealt with the pain all at once instead of suffer through it, then have to do it anyway."

I stared at him, in awe at his proposal, and then began to think. He stood and walked out of the cell, disappearing, once more, behind the wall. Since he made a right, I assumed that he was heading toward the basement again. I did not question him nor did I concern myself with his intentions.

I sat there for some time, thinking, before Sukata returned. When he entered the cell, he was holding a large, broken rifle stock, some bits of fabric, a piece of cardboard, some of the parachute cord, a table or desk leg, and a small chunk of wood. I knew what the items were for, but did not acknowledge how he intended to construct a prosthetic from the components. He set the items on the ground and said, "Think about it. I'll be on the other end of the building, trying to find a way out." With that, he left me be.

At first, I could not bring myself to consider removing my own leg but, then, I began to consider the benefits of removing the leg. I began to think that I could save Sukata and I, both, a lot of trouble, would be able to walk again rather than having to be dragged around, and would not have to suffer through the pain nearly as long. The pros to the situation were beginning to outweigh the cons.

While I was trying to decide, I heard something rustling beneath a rifle rack. I did not pay much attention to it at first, but then it began to become an annoyance. After listening to it, for what seemed to be hours, I decided I would try to investigate further.

Leaning over as far as I could, I managed to grab the edge of the rifle rack and began to pull it toward me. Once I had moved it approximately a meter, I could see a ventilation duct built into the wall. I could not see past the grate that covered the duct, but knew that whatever was causing the noise was getting closer to it.

Watching closely, as a child might watch an ant hill in curiosity; I could see the grate begin to move. Thinking it was Sukata, I said, "Sorry, that is not an exit," and began to chuckle at my joke. When I did not hear a reply, I assumed that he was having trouble getting the grate loose. I continued to watch, hoping that I would not have to crawl across the floor to aid him.

Eventually, the grate came free and a creature began crawling out of the duct toward me. I became voiceless...unable to speak...unable to yell...unable to move. In my mind, I was screaming at my body, telling it to move but, nothing seemed to work.

The creature made it out of the duct and to the edge of the rifle rack before my body responded. Immediately, I began to crawl toward the door, trying to get away. I ignored the pain that was shooting up my leg and the cracking and crunching noises it was producing as it floundered behind me.

I was nearly able to grab the frame of the door when the creature grabbed my right leg. The pain was intense, causing me to yell. I tried to rip it free from the creature as I pulled myself through the door. I continued to yell, hoping Sukata would hear me and come to my rescue.

I dragged myself through the doorway and placed my left foot on the frame of the door, trying to use it to shove off. I did not succeed but I did manage to get every part of my body out of the room with the exception of my right leg.

The bite was extremely painful. I had never felt anything like it before. I do not know if it was the combination of my leg being broken and the bite or if it was simply an exaggeration. I do know that is was the worst pain I had ever felt. It seemed as though a very large pliers grabbed my leg and tried to tear a piece of flesh from the bone.

Without hesitation, I began slamming the door on my leg in hopes of severing it. I felt that I could not wait until Sukata came; by that time I may have already been infected. I was not willing to take the chance of turning into one of those creatures if I could keep from it. Ultimately, the creature made my decision for me.

Sukata ran into the room and stopped. I yelled, "Help!" With haste he ran to the door and peered in. He knew, then, what I was attempting to do. He looked to me for approval. His stare was answered, "Do it! Do it! Do it!" With one strong swing, my leg separated just above the knee. I was relieved and depressed at the same time. I did not know how to react until the pain came and I passed out.

I awoke with Sukata watching me. The nub where my leg once was is bandaged and I am chained to a railing that runs along the wall. Judging by the wear on it, it must have been used to chain or leash guard dogs; I am not certain though. Sukata explained that he bandaged my leg and killed the creature in the room. He also explained that I would be weak for a while due to blood loss but, I should be fine. I gave him a thumb up and went to sleep.

I awoke later in the day, near dusk. Sukata was still watching me. When he saw my eyes open, he offered me the last piece of the beef jerky and said, "You should have it, you've had a 'shitty' day." I took the beef jerky without question and nodded in gratitude. He accepted my gesture and sat across the room from me.

I understood his actions and did not blame him. I agreed to the chain and his promise of killing me if he is able to. I enjoyed the beef jerky while I wrote this. This may very well be my last log so to whomever finds this: "Shut up and do whatever it takes to survive." ~Sukata

Keep your eyes open, take nothing for its face value, think before you do something, and above all find a good friend to watch your back as have I.

Log Entry 44

When I awoke, Sukata was unchaining me. I was confused by his action but he explained that he was going to find a way out of here. I told him I did not feel well and he said that it was most likely due to loss of blood. I did not believe that and explained that my thoughts were becoming chaotic and that I felt so hungry that I want to eat the leg that he had cut off. He responded by telling me not to worry; it will pass and that he was not going to give me my leg. I became angry and belligerent and began yelling. He simply ignored me and walked away, saying that he would be back to get me as soon as he found a way out.

That was some time ago. I have not heard, nor seen, Sukata since he left. I fear that he may have died, which is unlikely, or decided to leave me for dead. I feel myself beginning to hate him again; worse this time. I believe that he should die an ever so painful and agonizing death that shall rain upon him more pain than I have ever thought of feeling.

I feel extremely hot and I am sweating profusely. My body is shaking so bad, I am barely able to write. I do not know how much longer it will take to get through this; if I even survive…

I have decided that I will keep a record of any changes as the day progresses. It is early morning as of now and I feel as though my hunger is escalating. My body temperature is slowly increasing or it is getting hot in this building. My body is beginning to shiver as though it were cold. My thoughts are becoming more muddled with every passing moment.

It is midday now. I can feel myself losing control, slowly. My thoughts are becoming increasingly blank. I cannot remember much before I met Sukata. My heart rate is slowly increasing. I examined my nub, finding that it is turning a black-grey color.

It is midafternoon. My leg turned completely black at the nub and grey lines are spreading, like varicose veins, toward my hip and groin. I forgot everything before the military base; as though spotting the military base was my first memory. I am losing control of bodily functions. My thoughts are near

blank and I can hardly process words I read and write. I am

coughing blood.

It almost dark. Sukata not come back. Left me dead. Hope he

dies. Anyone finds this, I hope smart enough kil*(pen trails*

off page)

28551114R00176

Made in the USA
Charleston, SC
15 April 2014